Path of the Lion

Rising Kingdom

Part One: The Birthright

K.T. Brown

Published by Amazon KDP

Eight Nations of Shiveria

Nubariah

Sierra

Atlantica

North Pacifica

South Pacifica

Edia

North Arctica

South Arctica

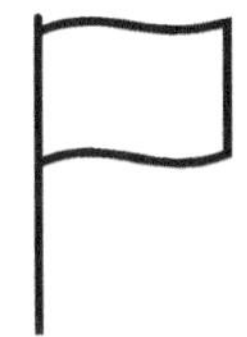

Clans of Nubariah

Lion Clan (Ouidah Territory)

Oph-Ur Clan (Aswan Territory)

Jaguar Clan (Mombasa Territory)

Wolf Clan (Hidden within the Walswe Mountains between Aswan and Mombasa)

Monk Clan (Genies Island between Atlantica and Nubariah)

Contents

To my sister Sholanda Johnson

Although you are not here to see the vision of this project come to life, I would like to thank you for pushing and inspiring me to create a project that will inspire those that look like us.

You will be forever missed and loved. May you sleep peacefully.

Prologue

A long time ago before the ancient days, the cosmos were created by the Supreme God Abiama. Out of his rib was Ala, the mother of wisdom and out of fire the angels were created. Twelve realms were created with different worlds uninhabited. Our world, Shiveria, was within the third realm where all terrestrial life were created. Before life took over the third realm, Shiveria was formless and dark. The moon was just a burning rock hovering over fire and brimstone.

Coming into the darkness like a flash of lightning were nine Shadow Lords with legions of demons. Chashak, self-proclaimed as the Lord of Darkness was their supreme leader. They were condemned by the Supreme after waging war against him in the cosmos. Chashak glared at the Supreme's fiery red eyes from the blazing darkness. This was a hell he was looking to one day escape from, or at least make it into his base when he prepares for a second war against the cosmos.

"I will one day cast my revenge and take the cosmos as the new Supreme God of the Cosmos," the Lord of Darkness said.

 After his declaration, the firmament shut behind him and his followers. There was no escape for the dark entities.

As time progressed Shiveria was formed into waters. The Supreme, with the help of his companion Ala divided the waters, creating the sea and sky. They created the sun for day and gave the moon it's light for the night with the star's assistance. Creatures from the sea were formed and the birds in the air were developed to reach the heavens. After the Supreme finished His job dividing the waters and creating the sun and moon, He created the land mass of Sahawayda. The grass sprouted from the dirt. Trees and bushes appeared. Every herb, vegetable, and fruit sprouted from the ground followed by the wild beasts, livestock, and insects. Then the Supreme formed mankind out of the brown clay and Ala breathed life into the man and woman. The man was given authority over all the creatures of Shiveria, the woman was his helpmeet. The man and woman became husband and wife and began to multiply with children. Then the Supreme rested and watched over the third realm and the rest of the cosmos.

Chashak, however, refused to be stuck in Hell. While Shiveria was ruled by mankind, the Lord of Darkness ruled in what he named Nether, the City of Fire. Him and the Shadow Lords heard of mankind and how Shiveria was formed into paradise. They all felt that the time was near to get their revenge. Chashak gathered the nine Shadow Lords into a ring within his council chambers plotting against mankind.

"Now is the time to destroy the terrestrials before they destroy us," the Lord of Darkness said.

"What will we do?" questioned Shadow Lord Mercius. "The terrestrials are invincible when they are together."

Chashak let out a malicious smile.

"You just answered your own question Lord Mercius," he said. "United the terrestrials are unstoppable. But if we can turn some of them on our side, then we will have an opportunity to destroy them all."

The Shadow Lords agreed and settled with the plan of dividing and conquering mankind. But once their plan was decided, the Shadow Lords had an unexpected visitor. It was the first man the Supreme created. Chashak snarled when the man appeared.

"What are you doing here terrestrial?" questioned the Lord of Darkness.

"I do have a name," the man said. "And my name is Chukwu, Grand Guardian of Shiveria."

"Well Grand Guardian, what is it that you want? Or are you here to destroy us already."

"Your time is not at an end yet. But don't think the Supreme can't see your evil doing. He is watching you. And if you do succeed in your plot, a mass portion of Shiveria will be yours including nine realms. But a portion of Shiveria and the remaining three realms will belong to the Supreme. Though you will be successful, your greed of wanting every portion of Shiveria and the remaining realms will be your destruction at the very end when my offspring destroys you."

Chashak sneered at the Grand Guardian, then grinned.

"Thank you for the foreshadow," he said. "I will make sure then that your offspring dies by my legion before the time comes."

Chukwu fell silent and turned away from Chashak and his lords. The Lord of Darkness watched as the

Grand Guardian disappeared from his world through a portal.

"Now is the time," Chashak said to the Shadow Lords.

The Shadow Lords entered the surface of Sahawayda. The place was of paradise. A great city was built with a solid gold gate around it. Mankind was at peace. There were at least 100,000 inhabitants with their father and ruler Chukwu sitting on the throne as their Grand Guardian. It was everything Chashak and the Shadow Lords heard of through reports.

Chashak spotted a woman sitting under a tree getting fresh air. He was very crafty with his vile imagination. He grabbed a cup from his cloak and dipped it in fresh water near a river that was clear as crystals. A tendril of black smoke came from out of his fingertip as he touched the water tainting it with a potion. Chashak disguised himself as an old man and walked towards the woman.

"Hello young lady," he said. "You look parched. May I offer you some water?"

The woman smiled at him in gratitude.

"Thank you," she said. "Me and my husband were on our way to explore the uncharted lands of Sahawayda and we decided to make a stop here outside of the city. I am parched but my husband is fetching us some water now."

Chashak stared at a man from the distance putting water in jugs. He turned back to the woman staring at her with deceptive innocence.

"I insist," he said. "Trust the words of an old man, you don't want to go on your long journey without quenching your thirst. No telling what's out there."

"You're right," said the woman. She shrugged her shoulders, "Why not."

The woman took the cup from Chashak and took a gulp of the tainted water. Her eyes opened up like the darkness of night.

"Wow, I never tasted water like this before," she said. "Can my husband try?"

"Yes, you can have it all," said Chashak.

The woman took the cup to her husband, and he drank feeling the same effect as his wife.

"My work is done," said Chashak in his dark voice.

The woman and man that drank the Lord of Darkness' potion was under his control as they were introduced to the Shadow Lords within the wilds of Sahawayda. The couple under the command of the Shadow Lords petitioned against the Grand Guardian as eventually a rebellion broke out which caused mankind to split. The rebels inhabited their own lands governed by Chashak and the Shadow Lords. They became known as the outer nations.

Chukwu's words were coming true. The Supreme gave Chashak nine realms of the cosmos and a mass portion of Shiveria after mankind had divided through corruption. But the Supreme kept the tenth, eleventh, and twelfth realms and divided the continents of the outer nations from Sahawayda. The Shadow Lords inhabited the nine realms and ruled over the dark worlds.

Sahawayda had split into two territories led by Chukwu. The other land became Nubariah which the Grand Guardian eventually became king after defeating one of the inhabitants for the position in one-on-one combat by the name of Ekwenzu. He became the top general for Chukwu until he rebelled against him which civil war broke out in the land. Chukwu defeated Ekwenzu and forced him to retreat to the outer nations.

Once time has passed, Chukwu was translated to the cosmos leaving his legacy to his new established bloodline, the Ezenwa family, to rule Nubariah from generation to generation as High Chieftain. Ekwenzu joined forces with Chashak in Nether after his passing vowing to destroy the bloodline of Chukwu. Ekwenzu's power translated back to Nubariah and was worshipped by the witch and the mask people in caves and was wielded by those he chose who he felt could oppose and challenge the High Chieftain.

The Shadow Lords eventually clashed with the lust of power having the desire to conquer each other's realm and territories. This caused them to split into two legions. The first four realms became know as the Shadow League led by Khonshu whose sole purpose was to conquer Sahawayda and the inhabitant land of Nubariah to prove his superiority. The last five realms formed as the Black Crow Society led by Scion, the son and descendant of Shadow Lord Xedohr, who continued to rule over the outer nations until this day patiently waiting for Khonshu's defeat by his enemies so he could stake claim as the Chief Prince of Shiveria and the cosmos next to Lord Chashak who would become its emperor.

The stage was set for the final battle at the end of time. The Shadow Lords were prepared for war while the prophesy was close of Chukwu's power entering the High Chieftain that would destroy Chashak and the Shadow Lords.

In Remembrance of that Beautiful Day

Within the palace grounds of Palasera, the capital of Nubariah within the Ouidah Territory of the Lion Clan, two brothers, Moses and Ramses, were face to face scowling each other. Ramses, the oldest child at the age of seven, was 6 inches taller than his brother Moses. Although he was only four years old, there was no intimidation coming out of Moses as he stared at Ramses' face with a focused look, ignoring the white outfit and colorful drapes surrounding his kaftan.

"I bet you can't defeat me," said Ramses. "Master Ngozi taught me a new technique.

"I don't care what he taught you," said Moses. "I'm not afraid of you."

"I'll make you go cry to mama when I'm finished with you."

"Shut up!"

Moses could feel the adrenaline pumping in his system as he saw his big brother poking his tongue at him. At the moment, he didn't care what Ramses learned at training school. He only imagined punching him in the nose, making his big head crash on the marble pavement. Moses wanted Ramses to cry to his momma full of tears with snot and blood hanging from his nose. Ramses would leave him alone then, were the thoughts that came through his brain. *That stupid head. I'll show him.*

He charged at his brother throwing a right hook. Ramses blocked his punch and shoved his head pushing him back. Moses began to wail while still throwing punches. Ramses continued to block his punches while mocking him, pushing him on the ground.

"Awe, what's wrong? You can't hit me?"

Moses screamed while tears rolled from his eyes. He tried to tackle his brother to get him off the ground, but Ramses moved out the way taunting him then threw him to the ground. Moses was fuming with rage, frustrated that he couldn't take his big brother down. He laid flat on his stomach and threw a tantrum, kicking his feet and pounding his fists on the ground.

"You are such a baby," said Ramses. "I didn't even hit you."

Moses got up to his feet and stomped, fists still clenched. The great rage within him continued, but a faint thought crept into the back of his mind like a revelation.

He might be bigger than me. He might be stronger than me. But one day I will be better than him.

Moses refused to punk out from the bully he saw as his big brother. He stormed towards him lifting his fist and throwing another punch to the stomach until a big hand jerked his arm that felt like sandpaper. Moses looked up to see Master Ngozi, the Lion Clan's greatest warrior and teacher scowl at him and his brother.

"That's enough you two," he said. "Stop this madness, what are you doing?"

"I'm sorry master, but Moses started it," said Ramses.

"I don't want to hear it Ramses. Today is an important day and you two want to horseplay?"

Ngozi glared at Moses while gripping his arm. The tears from his eyes dried up as he looked more alert at the martial arts master.

"What is wrong with you boy," Ngozi said. "All on the ground like that, you'll dirty up your clothes."

Moses got to his feet as Ngozi brushed his clothes.

"At least I see no dirt coming out. Now get inside, your parents expect you to be on your best behavior. Am I making myself clear?"

"Yes master," the boys responded.

The boys followed Ngozi inside the palace. Ramses stuck his tongue out at Moses as he rolled his eyes.

Big bully, Moses thought to himself. *One day I'll show you.*

Within the palace walls, guards were lined side by side in their armor with electro spears in hand. Moses and Ramses continued to follow Ngozi while looking around. Nobles with multi-colored royal dashikis roamed around the palace hall. Some of them the boys didn't recognize.

"Today boys is a day of unity," said Ngozi. "It took your father years to unite the clans of Nubariah. He managed to get most of our brother tribes to come here and unite, but for some reason, the Wolf Clan decided to stay hidden. We as a people have to embrace our pride. Here is a history lesson you must learn here boys: over centuries Nubariah has been full of life with technology no other nation in the world could fathom. Our infrastructures are made of fine gemstones, gold, iron, and other various minerals located within the caves outside of Palasera. How come you think this is our capital?"

The boys listened to Ngozi but at the same time listened in on two nobles' conversation that was walking past them.

"With all this technology we have our armies still using primitive weapons," one young noble said. "I mean we have the best technology that could advance civilization as we know it, but our military depends on some mystical power from a God we can't see."

Ngozi heard the young nobles' conversation as well and frowned.

"Master Ngozi," said Moses. "Why don't we use our technology?"

He firmly placed his hands on the boys' shoulders letting out a smile.

"Do not listen to those with little faith," he said. "There is hope in all situations. You see, we only use technology to help sustain the world from being tainted. In combat, however, we must channel our energy on the universal power that our ancestors have been embracing from the Supreme. The Lion is the most sacred clan in the world, and we must lead by example for the rest of the clans around the world."

Ngozi and the boys stopped when they saw their mother walking towards them. She wore a multi-colored dress with diamonds glistening, clanking in high heels. Her hair was wrapped in a head covering of silver diamonds matching her dress. The boys ran towards her and hugged her while she stooped down and let out a smile.

"You boys act as if you haven't seen me in days," their mother said.

Ngozi walked up to their mother and bowed to his queen.

"Your highness."

"Master Ngozi, greetings," she said. "I hope my boys didn't cause too much trouble for you."

"These knuckleheads? I had to stop their horseplay. They were getting way out of hand."

The boy's mother placed her hands on her hips with a disappointing look. The boys backed away with expressions of guilt.

"Ramses and Moses," she said. "I am highly disappointed in you. You two are the sons of the High Chief. Act like it."

"Yes ma'am," the boys said at once.

She glared at Moses and grabbed him by the arm examining closely a dirt splotch on his pants leg.

"And what is this?" she interrogated. "You stained your clothes."

She turned to face Ramses.

"What did you do?"

"I did nothing," said Ramses.

"You lie."

"I swear I didn't do anything Mother."

Moses stuck his tongue at Ramses with an "ah-ha, that's why you're in trouble". Ramses pointed his finger at Moses tugging on his mother's dress.

"See, he's starting it!" he yelled.

"No I'm not!" yelled Moses. "He starts it. He does it all the time!"

"Enough!" their mother yelled. "I don't care who started it. What's done is done. You two are brothers, now act like it. Do your father proud and apologize to each other."

Moses glared at Ramses watching him sway his body while placing his hands in his pocket. Without any words to say, their mother scowled at them with a warning of smacking the back of their heads. Moses felt as if Ramses should apologize. Apologize for being such a bully to him from the time he took his first steps, or possibly the day Ngozi and his father agreed to train Moses soon in the arts of the Kung Dambe, the Lion Clan's fierce and traditional martial arts. But to avoid his mother's harsh discipline, Moses had let out the words, "I'm sorry" hearing Ramses say it at the same moment.

Ngozi chuckled shaking his head.

"Boys will be boys regardless," he said.

Ngozi heard a beep in his pocket. He knew it had to be important. He reached into his pocket and pulled out the Optix, a hologram device made of optic stone that produces light for the caller to visually see the receiver. Ngozi pulled out the square-shaped device and clicked a button as a face of a man with a turban on his head appeared, Oba Ezenwa, the Chieftain of Nubariah.

"Yes, your highness," he said.

"Master Ngozi," the Chieftain said. "Take my family to the banquet hall at once. We are beginning soon."

"We will be there."

The Chieftain's face disappeared shutting off the device.

"The banquet is starting," Ngozi said. "We better get going."

The boys held their mother's hand as she followed Ngozi to the banquet hall. Ramses was ecstatic seeing a room of royalists from different clans and territories with each person dressed according to the customs of their clan. He was overjoyed to see the vastness of melanin distinguishing the vivacious feel of the room. However, Moses was inquisitive desiring the knowledge to know the culture in his presence. He examined the various colors each tribe had on their kaftans and suits. He tugged on Ngozi's pants leg getting his attention.

"Master Ngozi," he said. "Who are all these people? What do they have on?"

Ngozi let out a smile, proud to let the Chieftain's son know the great unity that was before their very eyes.

"What you see here is the Clans of Nubariah," he said. "The people in red and yellow robes represent the Monk Clan of Genies Island. They focus their power fully on spiritual energy. Their power is so great, that they can even train monkeys to aid them in battle."

Moses' eyes widened with fascination as Ngozi continued his teaching.

"The ones that are wearing fur around their kaftan represent the Jaguar Clan of Mombasa in Central Nubariah. They use their fighting prowess with swiftness, meaning their warriors always plan to finish their opponents as quickly as they can."

"How about the ones in the red and orange?" asked Moses.

"They represent the Oph-Ur Clan of Aswan. Since their ancestors chose the East Nubaran Desert as their home and training grounds, their warriors rely on solar power. They wield the power of fire given to them by the mystical fire guardians."

Moses nodded his head with approval and continued to walk alongside his mother, Ramses, and Ngozi as they ventured towards the crowded room and were met by the Chieftain. His outfit flashed the same colors as his sons and wife. The sapphire stone on the center of his turban gleamed from the light's reflection. Ngozi, Ramses, and their mother bowed to him. Moses watched and followed their example bowing.

"That is not necessary," the Chieftain said. "I'm glad you came on time."

"My apologies your highness, I lost track of time," said Ngozi.

"Save your apologies Ngozi. Have you heard anything of the Wolf Clan?"

"I tried for days reaching out to Alpha Akintoye, but he never responded."

The Chieftain rubbed his hand under his goatee in deep thought for a moment. He moaned in disappointment.

"Very well," he said. "Then we will continue without them."

Ngozi bowed to the Chieftain then left him to mingle with the other guests. Moses and Ramses wrapped their arms around their father's legs. He smiled at his sons and embraced his wife with a peck on the lips.

"You look absolutely beautiful," he said. "I pray we will be successful on this day."

"We will," his wife said. "I have prayed too. The clans have been hiding for too long. It's time for the clans of Nubariah to take a stand against the Shadow League."

"What is the Shadow League?" questioned Moses.

His mother looked at his father in a cautious glare as he smiled and placed a hand on his son's shoulder.

"Such a curious one, are you?" his father said. "You will grow up to be a wise man one day Moses. The Shadow League are bad people that want to destroy our people."

"But what do they do to destroy people?" asked Ramses hoping his father would give him the same compliment his brother received.

"Well, they rely on dark energy to conquer and wipe away their enemies. And that's why today the unification of our people begins. With Shadow Lord Khonshu gone we will bring peace to the Shiveria."

The Chieftain patted both his sons on their heads and turned back to his wife.

"It is important to step out of our fears Ashanti," he said to his wife. "I called this union for the sake of our boys. I know the Supreme has only chosen the eldest by right to be my heir, but I refuse for any of them to grow up in a future leading to darkness."

Ashanti kissed her husband on the cheek.

"Our children will not grow up in darkness," she said. "You have unified the clans of Nubariah. This unity will soon awaken the rest of the clans around Shiveria."

The Chieftain smiled and gestured her and his sons to follow him to the front of the banquet hall. Moses grabbed his mother's hand as they were greeting guests through the aisle. He saw a long table with the four clan leaders, three paired with their wives while one was paired with a young man, was in front of the room past the crowded guests. The Chieftain spotted Ngozi taking a seat near the table telling the boys to sit with him. Moses and his brother separated from their parents. He watched in officiousness as they greeted a man the size of a grizzly bear. His thick locs added to his intimidating size garbed in a burgundy dress suit with black suede shoes.

"Master Ngozi, who is that? wondered Moses.

"That is King Mongrel," he said.

"He's big."

Moses watched as his father and Mongrel bowed to each other with respect.

"Greetings Chieftain Oba," Mongrel said in a deep baritone voice that was unsettling.

"Greetings King Mongrel," the Chieftain said. "My goodness they said you were stacked in size, but it's amazing to actually see it for myself."

"Don't let his size intimidate you," said a woman sitting beside the king wearing a velvet red dress with a tiara made of diamonds on her head. "Deep inside he is a gentle soul."

"And I believe it to be true."

Drums started beating in the background with horns blowing. Everyone in the room was in complete silence after the drums and the horns stopped playing. Moses stood beside Ngozi as he watched his parents make their place at the table next to the rest of the clan leaders.

"Introducing Chieftain Oba of the Lion Clan and ruler of Nubariah," said one of the servants of the palace.

Moses peered around the silent room as everyone gave his parents their undivided attention.

"Greetings everyone and thank you for coming to what is a significant day," said Chieftain Oba. "For years the clans from abroad have been terrorized and plagued by the army of the Shadow League and the lords that rule it. The clans allowed the dark deity of

Chashak to bring fear in their hearts. Well, I say, no more. It is time to take a stand and fight!"

The crowd clapped and cheered on, moved by the Chieftain's words.

"Here I have three clans that decided to join our crusade against the Shadow League. King Mongrel and Queen Nabila of the Monk Clan take a stand."

The crowd stood up to their feet while people in the room were clapping. Moses and Ramses looked at a table across from them and saw two girls around their age wearing the same color dresses as the royal monk couple. The girls looked at them with blank stares. Ngozi smiled and placed his arms around the boys' necks.

"That is their daughters Tulip and Kalia," he said. "Don't just look at them. Wave and say hello."

Moses and Ramses smiled waving at them. The girls smiled back and returned waves of hello. The Chieftain continued his speech addressing the leaders.

"Chieftain Thuku and his son Prince Karungu of the Jaguar Clan take a stand."

The man stood with his son and waved.

"Chieftain Hullu and his wife Manunni of the Oph-Ur Clan take a stand."

The two stood to their feet joining the other leaders. A girl of long brown hair stood smiling at the couple in a dress that matched their outfits. She was slightly older than Ramses, but he couldn't help staring at her. He'd seen her before in passing while on family vacations to Nubariah's soothing beaches. His father introduced her one time. Aminnaya was the name he remembered. Her smile was bright like her golden-brown skin. He always had fantasies of her one day being his wife. Perhaps one day it could happen.

"With our clans united we will be able to reach out to the clans scattered abroad from the lands of the Atlantics, the Pacifics, and even the hidden polar regions of the Aquaic Clans," the Chieftain continued. "We must stay strong both physically and mentally. We must..."

The doors of the banquet hall flew open before the Chieftain could say another word. The crowd was startled and looked back towards the entrance. Uzoma, the General of the Lion Clan abruptly stormed in the room with a troubled look.

"My apologies your highness for interrupting," he said. "But we have a situation."

"What is it Uzoma?" inquired the Chieftain. "This meeting is important, but everyone's safety is just as important."

"It's the Shadow League. They came out of nowhere. They're here in Palasera led by the Shadow Lords."

The crowd began to panic as Ngozi grabbed Moses and Ramses by the wrists with a gloomy look.

"Listen you two," he said. "A great change is about to happen. No matter what, I need you two to stick by me. You understand?"

Moses and his brother nodded with sad approval while observing the chaos brewing around them.

"Well, it looks like they brought the war to us," said the Chieftain. He looked at the other clan leaders and smiled.

"I hope you brought enough warriors for this battle."

Chapter Two

Invasion

Pandemonium was beginning to build in the city. Moses could feel it. Or at least he thought he felt something disturbing. A sudden image flashed in his mind.

The clouds were black as smoke. The sky was grey as if the sun was sucked into the darkness of night. People were running as far as they could out of the city with solar cars crashing onto buildings and nearby palm trees creating mass chaos. Dark portals opened from the air to the ground leaving everyone in the street in terror. Out of the portal came an army of dark warriors. They were pale with red eyes. Their armor was made of rare metals that were black as night. The warriors were lined one by one as the Shadow Lords entered through one of the portals.

Two of them walked through the portal together, Shadow Lord Mercius and his wife Shadow Goddess Amaryllis. Mercius was of grey skin wearing a white drape with bronze linen. His crown contained three gold disks and his eyes were the color of the sun. Streaks of white lined through his cheeks matching the white stripes in his fiery red hair. Runes were tattooed on his arm matching the white streaks. Amaryllis was of coco skin with a long bob of hair as blue as the sea. A gold tiara was on her head draped in a long red dress showing her voluptuous physique.

The dark warriors bowed to them as they watched the city in amazement.

"Wow look at this place," said Amaryllis. "It is an ultimate paradise. My garden will definitely be a nice fit here."

"I'll have to admit we really outdid ourselves this time," said Mercius.

The streets were completely clear leaving dead silence on what was a beautiful day.

Shadow Lord Mercius gestured the warriors to arise and prepare for their attack on the palace as he and his wife marched forward. Mercius stopped everyone in their tracks staring at a sea of warriors at their opposition amongst the chaos. It was a total of a thousand warriors, two hundred and fifty for each clan.

"Do you see this my love?" said Mercius.

"They brought an army," said Amaryllis. "They knew that we were coming."

"There's no need to fret, we have the ultimate surprise."

Four sergeants of each clan made their way towards the Shadow army. Mercius stared coldly at the four men pursuing them. He wanted to immediately take them out with the thoughts of, how dare they decide to step up to me boldly. They must don't know that I'm a god. Amaryllis let out a sly smirk. The warriors were in pursuit without engaging their swords and spears. Their intentions were not to fight, not yet. Mercius nodded to Ameryllis as they walked towards the warriors in the middle of the abandoned street.

"Shadow Lord Mercius," said the Lion clan sergeant. "This is your only warning. Leave the vicinity of this place now or we will attack."

Mercius faced the Lion clan sergeant with an emotionless stare.

"Then prepare yourself, Lion," said the Shadow Lord. "For this is the day of your doom."

Mercius gestured his wife to come with him as he turned his back with strife on the sergeants. The Lion sergeant scowled at the other three sergeants and turned towards the army.

"Ready your arms!" he yelled.

Mercius and Ameryllis walked towards the shadow army. He stared at them coldly.

"Kill them all," he said.

"And leave no prisoners," said Ameryllis. "Or we could spare some of them. We could need the extra help once this place is for the taking."

"Engage," said Mercius turning to face the army of Nubariah's clans.

"Charge!" he heard the sergeant yell.

The Clan Warriors stormed towards the Shadow Army with their electric spears and swords drawn. Mercius' eyes glowed, gazing at his enemies. The Shadow Army followed pursuit drawing out laser swords. The armies clashed swords and fists. It was a mere one-sided affair Each clan warrior used both skill and power to take down the dark warriors. The warriors of the Oph-Ur clan used flaming swords and fireballs. The Jaguars used swift attacks with their energy ignited spears. The Monks used spears and pure energy from their spirits. The Lions used swords with their sacred power of the T'kaf, the purest form of energy. The uniting clans had the upper hand in the battle. Mercius watched as his warriors were being burned, slashed, stabbed, and blown away by energy beams. He peered through the battle and saw the sergeant pointing his sword in his direction. Their army was untouched. They stood flawlessly as the Shadow Lord and his wife backed away.

"Honey, what do we do now?" wondered Amaryllis.

Mercius looked at his wife then glared at the united army as they were in close pursuit with spears and swords pointed at them. Mercius smirked with his hands up showing signs of surrender. The warriors were puzzled as to why he would laugh at the face of death. Was it because he accepted his fate?

"Alright you got me," said Mercius. "I now wonder how your warriors will fair off against the other force?"

The warriors stared at each other in confusion. The Lion Clan Sergeant glowered at the Shadow Lord.

"Enough of your games Shadow Lord, it's over!" he yelled.

"Yes, it is," said Mercius.

A dark portal opened behind him, and a garrison of shadow warriors came out. Mercius and his wife turned around to face the portal. Out of the portal came out a muscular man of tan skin. His face was covered in a black iron mask matching the black hood covering his head that only revealed his red eyes. The dark warriors kneeled to him, and the Shadow Lord and Goddess bowed as the warriors backed with fear.

Back at the banquet hall, Moses gasped, feeling a horrendous dark presence. He could feel Ramses shaking him, telling him "Moses what's the matter?" But he was unsure. For the first time in his life, he was afraid. Moses trembled while letting out a whimper envisioning the terror the warriors were facing on the battlefield. The Shadows Lords were united ready to conquer with their army.

"You got to be kidding me," said one of the clan warriors. "That's Shadow Lord Khonshu. I thought he was dead."

"And their numbers are greater than ours," said a female clan warrior. "What do we do now?"

The warriors watched as more portals appeared. Dark warriors lined up behind the Shadow Lords in preparation for another attack. Mercius and

Ameryllis stood side by side next to Shadow Lord Khonshu.

"They are testing us," said the Lion Clan Sergeant. "But we cannot retreat. We must hold them off to stall more time for the others."

"I'll have to admit Lord Khonshu," said Mercius. "Everything you said is right. The clans of this region have rallied together."

"So you see it too," he said, his dark voice echoing through the mask. "The Lions are a bold clan indeed. I knew an opportunity like this would come. That's why I decided to wait for the moment to strike. They are hidden within the palace walls. We will push the army forward to strike. It is time to annihilate the remaining clans of Nubariah and put them to heel."

The Lion Clan Sergeant commanded the army to charge clashing once again with the Shadow army. The Shadow Lords watched coldly staring at the united clans as if they were not a threat.

"They are indeed strong united," said Khonshu. "But it's too bad they have to die so soon."

"Should we kill them so soon?" asked Mercius. "I mean this is quite entertaining."

"There's no time to make sacrifices for fun. Our target is the clan leaders and I care not to waste any time."

Khonshu let out his hands as two energy balls ignited glowing dark red. As the battle raged on, Khonshu released the energy balls forming them into one giant ball. They roared violently causing deep creases on the road, wiping away warriors from both sides. Their screams lasted only for seconds, then there was dead silence as their bodies disintegrated from the earth. Amaryllis laughed at the pain of the screaming clan warriors while Mercius stared emotionlessly as the giant energy ball created a mass explosion within the city quarter.

Moses whimpered with tears gushing out hearing the screams and cries of the warriors' souls. He could feel their suffrage and pain within the explosion. Moses saw as clear as daylight a mass crater within the city quarter with smoke and debris lingering in the tainted air.

"I thought you weren't going to sacrifice any of our warriors," said Mercius.

"That was a necessary sacrifice," said Khonshu. "Now let's get to the palace shall we."

Mercius and Amaryllis nodded their heads and followed Khonshu along with the Shadow army down the abandoned damaged street.

Everyone in the banquet hall was in a state of unrest, being told by royal guards to stay calm. Ngozi rushed towards Moses and Ramses at an alarming pace. He grabbed them both, looking at the Chieftain then bending down to face them. Moses wiped his eyes hoping Ngozi wouldn't spot that something is wrong.

"Listen up boys. I need for you to be strong. Right now, the city is under attack by the evil Shadow League. I need you both to stick by my side. I'm going to warn your father now so everyone can evacuate to the underground station before it's too late. Understand?"

Moses' chest was thumping, feeling his pulse beat rapidly. It was as he feared. What he was sensing was true. The city, his home, was in imminent peril. He nodded alongside his brother.

"C'mon," said Ngozi grabbing their hands.

Ngozi led the boys to their fathers until he saw Uzoma appearing in front of them. He figured Uzoma received the news of the warrior's annihilation due to his stumbling words. Moses listened closely to what the general was telling his father.

"Your highness," Uzoma said. "The… army… you sent…"

"Out with it Uzoma!" yelled Chieftain Oba with very little patience.

"They all have been wiped away by the Shadow League with ease."

The Chieftain gulped with the inability to breathe or say a word. The other three clan leaders were disturbed.

"That is impossible," said Chieftain Oba. "Our combined armies couldn't have been defeated that easily unless…"

Ngozi stepped in between the two with Moses and Ramses watching in curiosity and dismay.

"Your highness," Ngozi said. "I sensed it myself. The only warrior that could do such damage is Khonshu."

The Chieftain and Uzoma froze as the other clan leaders were stunned by the revelation.

"No, it can't be," said the Chieftain.

"Are you certain it's him?" asked Mongrel.

"You can't sense that?" questioned Ngozi.

All the clan leaders closed their eyes and sensed their surroundings. The dark energy they sensed terrified them.

"I'm guessing you all felt that too," said Ngozi. "It's no wonder our armies were effortlessly destroyed. Shadow Lord Khonshu is with them. Your highness our best bet is to gather in the underground station where it's safe."

Moses peeked around the room watching everyone murmur amongst one another.

"What is going on?" he could hear a young woman saying. "They're not telling us anything."

"The general looks terrified," said another woman. Please tell me we are not doomed.

Moses could sense the unrest that was surrounding him. The rambling within the room began to increase with the nobles' complaints about the warriors' failure. There were demands of using advanced weapons to take on the Shadow army instead of using primitive weapons. Uzoma turned to face the unsettled crowd.

"Everyone settle down!" he yelled. "We are working on the situation the best we can. Just be patient."

"But you are not telling us anything!" one of the nobles said.

"I bet the armies have failed," said a woman. "I say we use our high-tech weapons to take the bastards out!"

The crowd agreed as the clan leaders stared them down in hopelessness. Chieftain Thuku rose to his feet.

"So this is where things have come down to?" he wondered. "They have us surrounded as if they knew we were here. And all of you in here are so weak that you want to rely on weapons that will do little damage to their army."

"We must be patient and have faith," said the Chieftain. "It is not over yet. We will not use any advanced weapons."

"You sense that. Our armies have been decimated and they have brought their strongest leader. What can faith do to save us?"

Part of the crowd in the banquet hall agreed, nodding their heads.

"We still have soldiers and guards here as a garrison," said Chieftain Oba. "We can use them to hold the Shadow army from wiping everyone in here out. That way, we can get everyone out of the palace safely into the underground station as Ngozi has mentioned. Then the four of us can combine our powers and put a stop to Khonshu and the other Shadow Lords who are present."

Others in the crowd nodded, agreeing with the Chieftain's logic.

"That's madness!" Chieftain Thuku objected. "If the Shadow Lord can wipe out a thousand warriors all at one time, then what you think he will do to the rest of our armies? It is a waste of time."

"Then what do you suggest?" Chieftain Oba wondered.

"I suggest nothing. If you want to stand and fight, then that's on you. But I'm taking my warriors and my people out of here before disaster strikes."

"So you will take the coward's way out and abandon your brethren?"

Chieftain Thuku looked in the opposite direction in deep thought wondering if his decision was the right thing to do.

"Even if you leave Thuku," said Mongrel. "You and your people may escape. But don't think that the Shadow League will spare your people. Eventually, they will come after you. This is a perfect opportunity for us to combine our powers for their retrieval, but it's up to you."

"I'm sorry," he said. "I wish I had your courage, but I can't risk my warriors or my peoples' harm. Especially my son. He is my heir and the future of the Jaguar Clan. I'd like to thank you for inviting me to this summit Oba, but I must go. Good luck."

Chieftain Thuku and his son got out of their seats and walked out of the banquet hall to exit the palace. The nobles and warriors of their clan followed them leaving the rest of the clans to stand their ground.

"Anybody else wants to join them then there's the door!" the Chieftain yelled. "But I refuse to allow these tyrants to destroy what my ancestors built! I don't care what clan or history of your people you came from! If you allow evil spirits to take what is rightfully yours then your purpose is dead! Now if you're with me then we will follow through with the plan. And if not then leave and be on your own!"

No one in the banquet hall budged or made any kind of movement after the Chieftain's commands. Mongrel placed his hand on the Chieftain's shoulder.

"We're with you Chief," he said. "You're not in this by yourself."

"Then follow me," said the Chieftain. "We have work to do."

Dark Power

The Shadow Army marched forth towards the palace in full force past the crater full of the fallen warriors' ashes floating in the atmosphere. It was dead silence. Moses could feel their approach as his father commanded everyone in the banquet hall to follow his instructions of getting to the underground station below the palace. The feeling was surreal as the Shadow Lords led the army in unison with bloodshed on their minds. Khonshu and Mercius saw the palace from the bridge. Four tall pillars stood on the four corners of the palace grounds. They were getting closer. The taking of this kingdom was inevitable to them. Fear consumed Moses as he held on to his mother's dress. She smiled and lifted him off his feet while pressing a kiss on his cheek.

"It's okay baby," she said. "I'm here. We will be safe I promise."

Moses buried his head on his mother's shoulder feeling out the Shadow Lord's dark presence. Khonshu looked at Mercius.

"You know they expect us to break into their palace through force," said Khonshu.

"I guess they're more predictable than I thought," said Mercius. "They only know little of our power."

"Yes indeed. It's time for them to know why the clans fear the Shadow League."

Khonshu and Mercius paused, raising their arms. Their eyes flickered red. The air vibrated around them as if the wind knew of their evil vitality. Beams of energy shot out from their fingertips that were the size of pebbles in front of their army. The beams expanded into portals as the Shadow Lords walked into the portals followed by their army.

The guards of each clan led the nobles out of the banquet hall to the underground station. Ramses clanged on to his mother while she held Moses in her arms hoping he wouldn't lose her. Moses saw the nobles, both men and women scurry out of the banquet hall in panic with a few of them nearly bumping his mother. He looked down seeing that his brother was not trampled amidst the chaos that was brewing. Moses then turned and spotted his father talking to Ngozi and Uzoma at the table while the alarm sounded. He heard the last part of their conversation. Their exchange of words was something Moses would never forget.

"Make sure you take care of my family," the Chieftain said to them both. "In case I am gone that is your top priority. They must make it out of here for Nubariah to survive."

"I will devote my life to my duty," Ngozi said.

"So will I," said Uzoma.

The men turned and saw Ashanti and the children staring with wailing eyes. The Chieftain grabbed Moses from her and placed him next to Ngozi along with Ramses. He took his wife to the corner of the room and gave her a long kiss. Tears stained her eyes as he wiped them with his thumb.

"Do not cry for me my love," he said. "Your survival matters."

"I don't want to leave without you," she wailed. "I need you. Our sons need you."

The Chieftain grabbed her arms and stared into her eyes.

"Look, there isn't any time. If I don't make the necessary sacrifice, then the Shadow Lord will kill us all and all of Nubariah will be lost. Our boys are the next generation of this kingdom. It will be gone forever if they get taken out too. Stay strong and get out of here. Promise me you will."

She nodded faintly bending her head down. The Chieftain gave her one last kiss and gave her his farewells. "Goodbye my love." He crouched to the boys and hugged them. Moses wrapped his arms around his father's neck refusing to let go. He was afraid of what was going to happen next. He couldn't let go, but he had to. Ramses shed a tear hoping this wouldn't be the last time he would see his father. After a few moments, they let him go. He backed away to join the other clan leaders as they left the banquet hall. Uzoma placed his hand on Ngozi's shoulder and pulled him in for a hug.

"I wish you luck my brother," Uzoma said. He peaked at Ashanti, Ramses, and Moses then gave Ngozi a nod of approval.

"I will ensure the nobles get to safety," he said. "Make sure you watch after them for me.

Ngozi nodded placing his hand on Uzoma's shoulder.

"I will assure it," said Ngozi.

Uzoma jogged out of the banquet hall as Ngozi stepped to Moses, his brother, and Mother nodding his head to them.

"It is time to go," Ngozi said.

Ashanti sighed with grief as she grabbed her two sons.

"Then let us depart," she said.

Moses walked alongside his mother and Ramses as Ngozi led them out of the banquet hall to the palace hallway. He watched as his father stood side by side with King Mongrel and Chieftain Hullu amid the departing nobles.

"I assume the two of you gave your families farewells," Chieftain Oba said.

"I refuse to call it farewells," said Mongrel. "But I did speak to my wife and daughters."

"I have spoken to my wife and daughter as well," said Chieftain Hullu.

"Good," said the Chieftain. "Then let us proceed to the throne room. With our power combined it'll lead the Shadow Lords to us which will give a distraction for our people to escape."

The Chieftain pulled out his Optix to get in contact with one of his guards.

"Make sure every perimeter of the palace is guarded tightly," he said.

The Chieftain turned his attention to Ngozi. Moses stared as Ngozi and his father met each other halfway in the emptying hallway.

"Tell me what is going on Ngozi," he said.

Ngozi shut his eyes feeling his surroundings. He could feel the darkness pursuing them at this moment. The nobles were being led like a flock of sheep. The guards barricaded each entrance to the palace. He sensed the Shadow Lord's presence closing in with their army. There was no chance for escape, no hope for survival this day. Ngozi was hesitant to tell the Chieftain because of his pride and honor. But the moment was near, the moment of the inevitable. He was hesitant, but Ngozi had to tell the truth. The Chieftain would appreciate it.

"The Shadow League is closing in," said Ngozi. "I sense they are closing in. They are using their magic to infiltrate the palace."

The Chieftain gave Ngozi an alarming look then turned back to the Optix.

"Change that. Guard the perimeter near the door, hallways, and chambers," the Chieftain warned the guard. "They are attacking us through stealth. We must allow the nobles to escape safely. We cannot afford any losses."

"Yes, your highness," said the guard on the Optix as his face faded.

"What is going on Chieftain?" wondered Mongrel.

"Ngozi just informed me that the Shadow League is using their magic to infiltrate the palace," said the Chieftain.

"No, you can't be serious. Those bastards."

"Let's just pray our people will make it out of here," said Hullu.

There was a sudden pause as Chieftain Hullu closed his eyes with a gasp.

"Can you sense that? he asked. "Something is suppressing the atmosphere of the palace."

The Chieftain could feel that something was wrong. Nearing the edge of the hallway, Moses could sense his father's disturbance. His father knew that Chieftain Hullu was right. Something wasn't right in the atmosphere. The air around them started to suppress to the point where it was hard to breathe. The Chieftain went back on his Optix to check on the guards.

"What is your status?" he said.

No one answered. The Chieftain worried that his plan would fail. He waited too long. He looked at his family as Moses stared into his weary eyes.

"We better go back for the others," he said. "Ngozi, escort my family to the others immediately."

"You're not leaving so soon are you?" said a voice the Chieftain and Ngozi knew all too well.

Moses turned around and saw Shadow Lord Khonshu enter their presence from the dark portal. Moses was frightened of the being's dark red eyes and bulky muscles. He grabbed his mother's dress feeling her hand press him to her leg. He quivered with tears staining in his eyes. Chieftain Oba and Ngozi stepped in front of Moses, Ramses, and Ashanti facing the Shadow Lord in a tense stare-down.

"Shadow Lord Khonshu," said Ngozi. "I thought me and the High Chieftain drove you back to your darkness.

"It looks like you failed to finish me off," he said. "And by being in the presence of the four of you, I must say I am only half impressed of what I see. We already killed your guards. And your families, and your people… well just say they are being taken care of."

"Then we will have to show you what we are capable of," said the Chieftain.

Moses peeked at the Shadow Lord at the edge of the hall as his mother gestured him to keep walking. His eyes were caught by the Shadow Lord's as he quickly ran and placed his head on the drapes of her dress.

The clan leaders felt rage within themselves at what possibly happened to their families. Chieftain Oba let out his hand in front of his family staring with intensity in the Shadow Lord's eyes.

"Leave my family out of this," he said. "It's me and the chiefs against you. If you are as powerful as you say, then prove it to us. Unless you are a coward."

Khonshu scowled through his iron mask, but his anger was deceptive. It was like a hawk stalking its prey. The Chieftain could tell by his body language. He studied and anticipated any move the Shadow Lord would make. Mind games were being played. He trained for years in dealing with a warrior's patience. Khonshu was not going to break him.

"You may have been successful at defeating some more of our men," the Chieftain said. "But now you have us to worry about."

"I will make sure I'll end this quickly then," said Khonshu.

Khonshu backed away with a grin gesturing for the leaders to step forth looking to test their might against him. Moses peeked his head again, but Ngozi grabbed his wrist.

"What are you doing boy?" he said. "Stay close to us and quit your nosiness."

"Yes master," said Moses.

Ngozi held his grip on Moses as he gestured his mother and Ramses to make a right turn down the hall towards the elevator where the underground station was located.

"We're getting close," said Ngozi.

Moses turned his head slightly to see Ramses holding on to his mother's hand. They were close to the elevator, that was what Moses was hoping. He had never been to the underground station. Moses only heard of it from his brother a few times. He was petrified. This was a moment he thought he would never experience. Moses was hoping this was a nightmare or at least a reality he was hoping to be over. He felt a sudden stop looking up at Ngozi as he stood in hesitance staring blankly at the walls around him.

"Ngozi, why have we stopped?" questioned Ashanti.

Moses was unsure of his feelings, but he sensed a dark presence drawing near.

"We are in grave danger," said Ngozi. "We're too late."

Moses gazed at the textured walls as they began to turn pitch black. It was as if his pulse skipped a beat as crowds of people, from noblemen to warriors, to stonemasons, were appearing through the walls in each direction. It was chaos. They screamed in horror with their eyes full of confusion. Moses was claustrophobic of people towering over him. Ramses felt the same as he clung to his mother's dress. They could hear Ngozi telling them to stay close to him. The screams were growing louder. Bewilderment plagued the hallway. Moses was astonished by what was before him.

"We have been breached!" yelled Ngozi. "The whole damned city has!"

"I'm afraid they are more than that," said Mercius coming out of a portal in front of them. "What you see now are subjects for our new empire."

The crowd's screams continued as Moses and Ramses felt their mother's arms wrapping them tightly. The dark warriors came out of the walls with laser swords drawn. Moses quivered, wishing he could find a place to hide. But there was nowhere to go. He recognized some of the terrorized faces from the banquet hall who demanded to use high-tech weapons. Perhaps now would have been the right time, but it was too late. He was hoping the bravery and power of his father and Ngozi would save him. Then their enemies would go away forever.

"Take everyone near Khonshu and the Chieftains," said Mercius. "I don't want anyone to miss this.

The dark warriors led the crowd back to the side of the hallway where the banquet hall was located. Mercius followed. Moses was both terrified and claustrophobic feeling the body heat of people surrounding him. Ngozi stopped and bent down to Moses.

"Go to your mother," he said.

Moses nodded and ran to her as she wrapped her arms around him.

Ngozi turned and released combos of jabs and kicks powerful enough to cut off one of the dark warrior's circulation. He grabbed its' sword in midair and slashed each dark warrior one by one. The crowd began scattering while the dark warriors were distracted.

"Yes, Master that's it!" yelled Ramses.

Moses felt the adrenaline rushing through him. Ngozi was doing it. He was going to set everyone free from this temporary prison. Mercius watched, his arms folded with a stale look. A team of dark warriors grouped stalking Ngozi. His guard was up, anticipating the shadow warrior's next move. Ngozi knew he was outnumbered, but he had a duty. The sword he took was drawn. His legs were in position.

"Can't you see he's a distraction, go after the woman and children! Go after all the nobles and the other royal families!" yelled Mercius to his warriors.

Moses gripped his mother tight hearing Ramses wail while two dark warriors pursued them. *Father where are you?* he thought. Moses wanted to wail alongside his brother, but his fear overcame him to where the tears were held back. On the corner of his eyes, a band of dark warriors grabbed each person either jamming them on the wall or slamming them on the ground.

Ngozi shut his eyes ignoring the army of dark warriors that were present.

"No!" he heard the Chieftain yell. "Let my people go! This is our fight, not theirs!"

Ngozi channeled his Tkaf and backflipped in midair decapitating the dark warriors that pursued the Chieftain's family.

"Enough!" yelled Khonshu from the other end of the hallway. "It is pointless to waste our warriors on the likes of the Lion Clan master. He will be dealt with soon. Just take the people and place them on each side of the walls."

He turned to face the three clan leaders gazing his eyes at Chieftain Oba. The crowd was completely silenced, forced to split in two leaving a space for the deciding battle that would change the history of Nubariah. Moses held on to his mother quivering as one of the dark warriors pointed a sword at them.

"Sit on that wall and keep quiet," it said in a dark raspy voice.

Moses could hear his mother telling him and Ramses, "It's okay loves. Sit down with mommy."

Moses sat alongside his mother and brother. The hallway was in complete silence. He turned and saw the Shadow Lord still face to face with his father and the other chieftains. The battle has not begun.

"I must say your warriors are impressive," said Khonshu looking at Chieftain Oba. "I'm impressed by this one. He should've been your general. And speaking of such, I have an additional guest in our celebration."

Uzoma came through one of the walls with two dark warriors walking beside him with swords in their hands. Amaryllis walked through the walls behind him with a malicious smirk. She had a dagger in her hand pointing it at his back. She and the dark warriors escorted him to the side of the wall facing Ngozi. Uzoma and Ngozi's eyes locked. Failure was in Uzoma's eyes, but empathy was with Ngozi's.

Moses watched as Ngozi met Mercius face to face as the hallway cleared.

"Everything is going to be okay my loves," Ashanti said to her boys. "I promise you everything is going to be okay."

"Don't think you will get away with this," Ngozi told the Shadow Lord. "I will make sure you see your defeat today."

Mercius stared into the eyes of Ngozi showing no signs of emotion. His gaze was cold, calculating in wait for Ngozi to make his move. Perhaps this is their style of fighting, manipulation, were the thoughts

Moses had as he saw Ngozi's bravery against the hideous-looking Shadow Lord. He had never seen such beings that were as cold-hearted as the Shadow League. Mercius smirked and backed away.

"You are a strong warrior Master Ngozi, I sense that," said Mercius. "But for now, let's enjoy the show and see what your fierce leader has to offer against the leader of the Shadow League."

What kind of sick game are these monsters playing? thought Ngozi. *Why they won't fight us? The bastards must be stalling. It's a trap.*

"Looks like our audience has settled down," said Khonshu turning back to the leaders. "I wonder where your families in the crowd are?"

"Enough!" yelled King Mongrel, his voice giving off a thunderous sound. "You will fight us or die right where you stand!"

The Chieftain used his arm to block Mongrel from attacking. He had to be patient and stick with the plan of combining their powers if they were to stand a chance against Khonshu.

"Do not let him get to your head," he said. "We will strike together."

The two other leaders nodded their heads in response and focused on their enemy. Ngozi scowled at

Mercius and joined Moses, Ramses, and Ashanti on the wall. Mercius and the dark warriors also cleared the aisle and joined Amaryllis on the walls further down. Moses watched, hoping his father would lead his nation to victory.

Chieftain Hullu drew a sword and ignited it with fire. He stooped low, placing the sword above his head. A fire glowed around his body. His eyes turned bright yellow. Mongrel pulled off his jacket and got into the monk's sacred position stooping down with his arm stretched far from his chest. He let out a long grumble, his deep voice carrying in the dense atmosphere. Chieftain Oba stooped with his legs spread. One hand was stretched, the other was pumped into a fist. He channeled his energy, aiming towards the head and chest of Khonshu. They dashed towards Khonshu all at once with power strikes. The Shadow Lord read their moves and blocked each strike as if they were light punches. Chieftain Hullu cut his flaming sword into the air igniting a fire arch that flung at Khonshu's neck. He ducked as another one hurled at his legs. He flipped out of the way but was hit in the chest by Mogrel's massive hand. He flew back towards the end of the hall landing on his back.

Khonshu quickly rolled back to his feet and was face to face with the Chieftain.

"So now I get to see what the Lion Clan Chieftain is made of," he said

Moses watched his father while gripping his mother's hand. "Go get him fatha," he said. He gazed at his father's fighting stance as he rushed an attack feigning a punch. Khonshu studied his movements closely despite the Chieftain's flash motion. He blocked the punch and deflected more of his punches and kicks. The Chieftain moved to a point where the crowd couldn't see him. Moses watched in amazement of his father's supernatural abilities. Khonshu formed into a dark tornado and got on his knees and meditated, sensing out his opponents. Hullu slashed his sword on the ground in the direction of Khonshu. A trail of fire scurried towards the Shadow Lord. Khonshu opened his eyes and released an invisible shield to keep the fire away. Chieftain Oba came from behind with a mid-kick aiming at Khonshu's temple. He turned and grabbed the Chieftain's ankle. Mongrel released a chop towards Khonshu's head, hoping to split it open.

"Get 'em, daddy!" Moses heard Tulip screaming. He smiled hoping the big man would beat him down.

The Shadow Lord caught Mongrel's chop effortlessly with his other hand. Hullu plunged his sword at Khonshu's stomach igniting the flares to the flame. The Shadow Lord's shield glowed dark red blocking the sword. Hullu struggled to pierce through the shield, pushing his sword with all his power and might. Khonshu pushed the three leaders away through the shield's power as they slid on the floor.

No, fatha, thought Moses. The words couldn't escape despite the protection he felt from his mother and Ngozi.

Ramses watched across from him seeing Aminnaya cling to her mother. If only he was strong enough to fight these monsters, then he would be her chivalry. He would take her away from here and profess his love for her. But he was helpless, trapped in a corner with no escape. His father and the other leaders were struggling against the Shadow Lord despite their combined forces of incredible power; Chieftain Thuku had coward away from the fight; then Uzoma failed to take the nobles, including his mother, little brother, and himself to safety. It was hopeless for him. But he had hope for his father, he and Moses had faith.

Moses and Ramses watched as their father rose back to his feet. Mongrel and Chieftain Hullu were also on their feet back in their attack position. They surrounded Khonshu refusing to back down despite his deadly power.

"Your highness!" yelled Ngozi. "Channel his energy, he's holding back!"

"He's right," said Hullu. "His power is incredible."

"But he hasn't seen anything yet," said Mongrel.

"Remain focused," said Chieftain Oba. "Ngozi is right, Khonshu is holding out on us. We must be cautious of his scheme."

Shadow Lord Khonshu peeked at Mercius and Amaryllis. Mercius nodded his head as the lips of Amaryllis curled into a malicious smile. Khonshu sneered and stood in place.

Mongrel felt his spiritual power manifest and assaulted his foe with all his might. He ignored the Chieftain's warning as he yelled, "Mongrel wait, he's luring you in!" But he was drawing close. He felt the adrenaline running through his veins thinking of all those threats the Shadow Lord made to his family. He was a father despite the title he was given. He had a duty to protect his people, his wife, his children.

Mongrel was close to his target, his fists pumped with the motive to shatter the Shadow Lord's bones.

Khonshu leaped at a speed that formed him into wind. Mongrel missed his target again this time shattering the walls in front of him after the wind was unleashed from his punch.

"Damn it!" he grunted.

The wind blew past Chieftain Hullu and Oba. Men and women behind them were screaming while covering their children. Chieftain Oba could hear thuds behind him after the screams, then silence. His blood boiled, hoping the Shadow Lord didn't kill innocents. Then he heard a quivering grunt beside him. He turned and saw Hullu's eyes widen, his mouth seeped out blood. Khonshu's fist was stamped on the Oph-Ur Chieftain's chest after appearing from the wind. A red glow came out of Khonshu's fist that released an energy blast through Hullu's chest. Khonshu pushed Hullu a couple of feet as he slid and lied motionless on the marble floor leaving a trail of blood smeared.

The room was full of silent mourns as Manunni and Aminnaya let out screams and wails of sorrow from the distance.

For the first time, Moses had witnessed the Shadow Lord's power. It was of terror. Ramses could feel the pain Aminnaya felt. Tears stained his eyes, rolling down his cheek like a stream.

The Chieftain and Mongrel were in disbelief staring at the lifeless body of Hullu. The feeling was as if losing a brother. Hullu was now gone, his spirit left his body. It was nothing they could do but continue their battle as the crowd watched on. The people of Nubariah were depending on them, so they had to continue their defense against the Shadow League.

The Chieftain and Mongrel placed their focus back on the Shadow Lord studying him closely. In unison, they directly attacked the Shadow Lord without second-guessing. The Chieftain and Mongrel used swifter combos to try and take down Khonshu with multiple combos in their fighting styles. The Shadow Lord dodged their moves continuously. Khonshu read their moves closely, seeing another opening for another attack. He saw his next victim vividly. Khonshu formed into another tornado. The Chieftain and Mongrel were on their guard.

"He's forming into another tornado," said the Chieftain.

"I see that," said Mongrel.

"Stay on your guard and use your senses. Focus on his movements."

Mongrel nodded, focusing on the energy of his opponent. A strong wind blew past Chieftain Oba. Mongrel turned watching nearly losing his breath as the Chieftain took a step back shielding his face and waistline.

"Oba!" Mongrel yelled.

The wind cleared. The tornado disappeared. The Chieftain let down his guard unharmed. Khonshu did not touch him. He turned to Mongrel and saw the Shadow Lord stooping in front of his massive body.

"No!" yelled the Chieftain.

Mongrel glanced down and felt a kick on his stomach knocking the wind out of him. His vision blurred. He could barely breathe.

The crowd was gasping as the Shadow Lord stood in front of him. The Chieftain tried to save the Genies King, but the Shadow Lord leap kicked him under his chin enough for his neck to snap. His body was in mid-air until he landed on the floor leaving cracks around him from the impact. Queen Nabila, Tulip, and Kalia were in dismay, staring and letting out cries of his motionless body. Moses watched from across hearing their screams. He could feel their pain, their sorrow. Moses could tell everyone around him was grieving.

The Shadow Lord cackled lifting his arms, presenting everyone in the palace halls his dominant power.

"Are you not all entertained!" he shouted. "Soon you will all see me as a god!"

"You are notin' but a bastard, devil!" screamed Queen Nabila.

Ramses placed his hand on Moses' shoulder as they watched in grief of the fallen leaders. Then they looked at their father, the last warrior and chief to step up against Khonshu. Moses knew of his father's wisdom. Ramses knew about his father's strength. He has to win this fight. Their nation depends on it. They watched as Khonshu stalked their father as if he was ready to devour his prey.

"C'mon father please," said Ramses.

"We're depending on you," said Moses.

"And then there's one," said Khonshu. "I've saved the best for last I hope."

The Chieftain did not respond to Khonshu's harsh words but only let out a fuming stare. The two gaped at each other in a showdown. It was now a one-on-one fight.

Chapter Four

On That Fatal Hour

I know it is a reason why you are the one of the greatest Chieftains of the Lion Clan," Khonshu said. "Legends say that the Grand Guardian chose your bloodline because of their pure spirit and might. The powers of the Lion Clan are sacred compared to all the clans of Nubariah and across the world. Show me Chieftain Oba your full power of the T'kaf. Show me your full strength of the Kung Dambe."

"So be it," said the Chieftain.

He planted his foot and clenched his fist feeling his knuckles popping. The gravity within the room started to thicken the atmosphere leaving everybody in the hallway uncomfortable. Moses and Ramses gripped each other tight, locking arms ignoring the heavy air that was bound to crush their small bodies. Their mother stooped, wrapping her arms around them, gesturing to them that their father was going to be fine.

"Be careful my king," she whispered.

The gravity within the hallway began to shift towards the Chieftain relieving the innocent people that were trapped by the dark warriors. Static electricity popped out of the floor. Moses quivered, yet he knew this power was of his fathers. *You can win Fatha*, were the thoughts that suddenly appeared in his anxious mind. *Please win.*

"Master Ngozi get everyone out of here, now!" yelled the Chieftain. "The Shadow League will be pulling back! I know they won't be able to handle my power before them!"

"Yes, your highness," Ngozi said.

Moses watched the Dark warrior in front of him turning away. Relief was the feeling he felt hearing the cry of Shadow Lord Mercius to his warriors.

"Retreat! We will deal with our prisoners once we escape these walls."

Moses watched as Mercius and Amaryllis created a round dark void towards the end of the hallway. It looked similar to the black walls to where the people came through terrorized. He watched as the Shadow Lord and his companion scurry alongside their warriors. He didn't know whether to be frightened or relieved. Moses could see the confused looks on everyone's faces. He heard the murmurs of people wondering what's going to happen next. He turned to see Ngozi rushing in the middle of the hallway as the people gained his attention. Moses hoped this nightmare would end soon.

"Alright, listen up," said Ngozi. "Whoever in here are warriors, no matter what tribe, stand before me now."

There was silence. All that was heard was the supernatural flare of the Chieftain's power. Uzoma peaked his head from the crowd and walked towards the spiritual leader. He placed his hand on Ngozi's shoulder, nodding that he will fight with him. Then another voice called out.

"Master Ngozi!" yelled a man with a shaven head with a black goatee.

He came out of a sky-blue portal alongside a few warriors matching his burgundy monk robes of yellow linen. He bowed to Ngozi.

"I am Monk Master Keno. We are at your service to protect the people."

Ngozi nodded and bowed to the Monk Master. He looked ahead of Master Keno and saw a vast number of Monk warriors appearing behind him. Moses was amazed by their count. Perhaps it was hope after all. He watched as Ngozi gathered the warriors.

Keno joined Ngozi and General Uzoma in front of the warriors, using their life force to create an invisible barrier that would protect the people from the heavy gravitational force in the hallway. Moses felt lighter despite the burden of his inner thoughts. He saw Ngozi gesturing him, his mother, and his brother to come. Ashanti grabbed him and Ramses' hand.

"C'mon boys," she said. "We can't let Ngozi out of our site."

Moses walked alongside his mother and brother watching the crowd follow the warrior's lead. Women were holding on to their children while the men walked alongside them. The children were either silent or wailing from their terrifying experiences. Moses turned and saw Tulip and Kalia sobbing while their mother gripped them. Their sobs were grievous. Tulip could barely walk, nearly fainting. Two monks escorted her while murmuring her words of comfort. Moses could feel their grief. If only he could give each of them a hug.

Ramses turned and saw Aminnaya and Manunni standing beside him with sobs and shudders. He forgot how beautiful Aminnaya was up close. Seeing her pain heated his desire for wanting to protect her with the same embrace his father had for his mother. He let out his hand, her eyes catching his.

"I'm sorry what happened to your father," he said. "But I want to let you know that you are not alone in this."

She smiled wiping tears from her eyes while sniffling snot.

"Thank you," she said taking his hand.

Aminnaya and her mother walked ahead. Ramses wished he could never let her go.

"Let us depart now!" said Ngozi.

Sparks from Chieftain Oba's power increased from the floor to the walls.

"Why are you all still here!" screamed the Chieftain. "Do as I say now Ngozi!"

"Yes, your highness."

Ngozi followed the Chieftain's orders leading everyone out of the palace alongside Uzoma, Keno, and the monk warriors. Moses and Ramses took a final look at their father in amazement. They glimpsed at the electric sparks levitating through his body. His turban floated from his head unwrapped revealing his fade top. Shadow Lord Khonshu was alert to the power that was wielded in front of him, Moses could tell.

As Moses followed everyone out of the palace, the Chieftain focused on a weakness to take away the Shadow Lord's defenses. His mind was focused on his target to where time stood still.

"You terrorized my people," he said. "You slaughtered my warriors. If you think you can walk in here and take my kingdom, then you have another thing coming!"

Chieftain Oba aimed for Khonshu's rib cage, dashing towards him with speed like lightning. The Shadow Lord was astonished but blocked the Chieftain's jabs. Khonshu felt a kick on his leg, catching himself from losing balance. He backed away, catching his guard to avoid any deadly blows the Chieftain was throwing. Khonshu closed his eyes, sensing his opponent.

"Gotcha," he said.

Khonshu grabbed the Chieftain by the collar and threw him to a nearby wall. The Chieftain used his quickness pressing his feet on the wall to summersault to the floor. He got back into his fighting position. Khonshu cackled, staring at the sparks flying visibly through the Chieftain.

Ngozi, Uzoma, and the monks led the crowd to the entrance of the palace with swords and electric jhspears wielded. Moses followed closely staring at the corpses of guards and warriors lying in pools of blood near the entrance. The feelings of disgust and nausea entered him. Moses was petrified. He felt his mother hold on to his small hand in a tight grip. She grieved to see the warrior's bodies.

Ngozi opened the doors of the entrance revealing the dark sky of clouds that brushed the air like smoke. It was a sight that Moses found unimaginable. He watched as Ngozi and the warriors rushed through the doors with caution. Moses felt his mother dragging him, commanding him and his brother to walk up. Moses felt the warm tainted air hoping freedom would be with them from the Shadow League's grasp. He hoped his father destroyed the Shadow Lord after the terror he brought on the people. Moses hoped Mercius and his men would disappear forever from the face of the earth, if only it was possible.

Then there was a pause. Moses could feel rapid heartbeats. He heard gasps and saw people around him backing away. His mother gripped his hand taking a step back.

"No, this can't be," she whispered.

Moses peeked his head past Ngozi seeing Mercius and Amaryllis standing in front of them with the

Shadow Army lined behind them ready for a command to strike.

"I hope you're not planning on leaving so soon," said Mercius. "We were just planning on picking up where we left off."

Moses could tell Ngozi and Uzoma were on full alert. Usually, he would be told to stay close, but there was a distance. A silent tension filled the atmosphere.

"Warriors prepare your arms!" yelled Uzoma.

The monk warriors assembled beside Ngozi, Uzoma, and Keno. Moses looked around the crowd seeing the fear on each person's face.

Mercius smirked then scowled.

"Kill the warriors and the rest of the royal families," he said. "Shackle the rest as prisoners."

The dark warriors darted at the people ready to feed their laser blades into the blood of those they would encounter. Uzoma commanded the warriors to attack, protecting the remaining members of the royal families, nobles, and natives. Keno fought side by side with Uzoma and Ngozi striking each dark warrior they came across. Moses watched as the monks fought gracefully against the dark warriors. Ngozi stood side by side with Uzoma and Keno forming a semi-circle to block the dark warriors from hindering the crowd. The monks slashed each of them with electro spears while blowing them away through their spiritual energy of blue light and wind. Ngozi and Uzoma defended themselves creating golden auroras on their swords from their energy. Each dark warrior fell effortlessly by their swords with their blood the color of black cherry spilling on the pavement.

Mercius and Amaryllis stood still watching their warriors fall. The Shadow Lord raised his right hand while his eyes glowed. The dark warriors ceased, standing in the opposition of Ngozi and the warriors that fought beside him.

"I have to say I'm highly impressed," said Mercius. "You truly live up to your reputation Ngozi. The Chieftain chose you well. But understand this. You and your men do not stand a chance against my army. So, my only warning to you is to stand down, and I promise you will be spared."

Ngozi scowled at Mercius then turned to face Moses and his family. Moses frowned clutching his mother's hand.

"You can beat him Master Ngozi!" yelled Ramses.

Ngozi nodded his head and turned back to face the Shadow Lord. Mercius and Amaryllis nodded at each other with malicious sneers.

"So, what is your decision?" questioned Mercius.

Ngozi let out a glare, pointing his sword in the Shadow Lord's direction.

"If you think I'm going to bow to you as a willing slave, then you are mistaken. Your blood will be on my blade Shadow Lord."

Mercius glowered and signaled his warriors to attack.

"Then I guess you will die," he said. "A pity."

He and Amaryllis' eyes glowed bright red as a dark portal opened on the ground. Dark warriors emerged by the dozens. Ngozi signaled the men back into attack position with their swords and spears drawn. The fight was going to become overwhelming, but

Ngozi was ready. He was not going to back away like a coward. If he was to see death this day, so be it.

"Make them an example!" yelled Mercius.

The dark warriors gathered and assaulted the warriors. Ngozi and the warriors held their ground ensuring the dark warriors wouldn't get past their defense. Their powers combined spilled more dark blood, but the task of defeating the Shadow League was tougher now that their portals were opened.

Amaryllis scanned through the crowd and gazed at Moses, Ramses, and Ashanti with evil intentions coming to mind. Moses caught her eyes, glaring this time, swallowing his fear. He had faith Ngozi would defeat them. His faith was with his father as the fight against Shadow Lord Khonshu made its way to the throne room.

The throne room was massive with an aisle leading to a flight of stairs where the throne stood. Corpses of guards laid on the ground in each corner of the room. The Chieftain and the Shadow Lord attacked each other with multiple strikes down the aisle. They were evenly matched, unable to land a punch. Khonshu paused, studying his opponent.

"Your power is indeed something," said Khonshu. "I'm highly impressed."

"You haven't seen nothing," said the Chieftain.

He dashed towards the Shadow Lord using rapid low kicks in an attempt to sweep the Shadow Lord onto the hard floor. Khonshu backed away at careful angles avoiding getting knocked down. With an attempt to slow the Chieftain down, Khonshu threw a jab to his chest. The Chieftain blocked the jab, his power vibrating through his body. The impact of their attacks caused the walls and floor to crack causing massive quakes. Moses could feel the fierce battle within the palace. If only he could witness it.

Moses saw in front of him that the battle turned for the worse. The semi-circle that was formed to protect him and the people was broken after one of the monks was stabbed to death in the stomach. The monk fell lying in his pool of blood. The dark warriors took advantage, slashing their blades into a few more monks. Ngozi screamed in sorrow at their deaths. Uzoma and Keno stood beside him holding their defense.

No, this is not happening, ran the thought of Moses. Ngozi and the warriors were unstoppable through their combined powers of spiritual energy. Despite the number of warriors the Shadow League had, he would've thought they would hold their ground because of their incredible power.

Ngozi and the warriors did everything they could to keep the dark warriors away from the crowd. The remaining monks assembled beside Ngozi, Uzoma, and Keno ripping through the massive army in unison while wielding their power. Keno glanced at Ngozi.

"Master Ngozi, we must push them back through our channeled Ki to slow them down," he said.

Ngozi nodded throwing the laser blade at the last corpse he spoiled. Keno and the monks placed their spears back on their holsters. Uzoma sheathed his sword. The dark warriors raised their blades aiming at their clear targets. The warriors channeled their energy creating a wave swarming their bodies. Their knees were bent with their palms out. The striking blow of the dark warriors was near their reach. Ngozi and the warriors released the wave of energy in a flurry, pushing the vast army away. Moses was amazed watching the dark army scurry while a few floated in midair after the impact. The dark warriors regrouped, giving Ngozi and the warriors spare time to lay out a plan.

"This battle is not ours for the taking," said Ngozi.

"Giving up so soon Master Ngozi?" wondered Keno. "We were just getting started."

"We have no choice. We are outnumbered. All of our warriors have been decimated. The more we stand our ground, the more likely we all die with our people enslaved. The Shadow League may take our land, but if they cannot take the people, then their efforts will be for nothing."

"Then we will need an evac at once before it's too..."

Then it happened. A blast, the sound of a laser beam, zipped in an instant in the direction of the crowd. Moses looked in the direction of Queen Nabila as she looked down and saw a bloodstain on her stomach. He screamed, feeling pain as if it was his mother. The feeling hit nearly home watching Tulip and Kalia scream in horror. Queen Nabila fell on her knees, blood seeping from her mouth.

"No, your highness!" bawled Keno running to the crowd.

He tried to pull her to safety, but another round of laser bullets flew through her chest leaving her body lifeless as she drew her last breath. Keno released a blue forcefield around the little girls, preventing the laser bullets from hitting them next.

More rounds of laser bullets flew as Moses crouched while flinging his mother's arm. He heard Ramses shriek turning to see blood oozing out of Manunni's mouth as it dripped on the marble ground. Her daughter was shot multiple times from the laser bullets, leaving her inanimate.

"Aminnaya!" yelled Ramses reaching out his hand.

Manunni fell on her knees blackening out to her death. The nobles of the Oph-Ur clan were all in trepidation seeing the rest of their leaders gone, both the queen and princess.

Ramses turned and saw smoke coming out of a wrist-wearing laser launcher from one of the dark warriors. Ramses' fear transformed into rage. He felt his heart-shattering in pieces. The potential wife he thought he would have someday had now become a painful memory. He was told he wasn't ready for combat but at this moment he cared less. Ramses shrieked, tears welling in his eyes. He yanked his arm, letting his hand loose from his mother's, and stormed towards the dark warrior his fist pumped. Ashanti had let go of Moses' hand rushing to go after Ramses. He was close to killing the monster that slain the girl he loved, who he thought he loved. Ashanti tackled Ramses on the pavement before he got any closer. He struggled to break free.

"Let go of me!" yelled Ramses.

"No, you'll get yourself killed," said Ashanti.

"I don't care, let me go!"

"Listen to me Ramses. Please, you must son."

Moses looked up and saw a blue forcefield surrounding the crowd. He saw in the midst Keno unleashing his power to protect the people from the dangers of the Shadow League. If only he could've done this sooner. Blood leaked from his nose. Moses saw that the monk was struggling. This was his last stand. He was the survivors' only hope. Moses hesitated, turning his attention back to his mother and Ramses hoping they were not the next victims of the

Shadow League's attack. He spotted them on the ground struggling. Moses rushed in their direction nearly feeling breathless.

"You are still young," said Ashanti. "You will one day find love. But what's important is you still have your family. Your father is still battling for us."

"But it's not fair," said Ramses. "Why so many people have to die?"

"I know my sweet, I know."

Ashanti wrapped her arms around Ramses. Moses felt relief, watching his mother and brother embrace each other. His mother turned and looked at him. She opened her arms for him to come. Moses walked to her as she embraced him. Tears rolled from his eyes thinking of all the lives lost and the people's suffrage. For the first time since the banquet hall, he felt safe. At least for now. Moses felt Ramses wrap his arms around him and his mother in a group hug. Then there were screams.

"Ngozi!" yelled Keno. "When is evac coming? I can't hold this shield any longer!"

Moses turned his attention back to the shield. The blue glow it once had begun to darken. How could this be? Who would be powerful enough to tamper with the monk's shield? He saw ahead of him Amaryllis' hands glowing dark yellow, swirling them at the shield.

No, he thought letting go of his mother and brother.

"We are preparing you shuttles now," said a man on the Optix Ngozi held in his palm.

"Just hang in there Keno!" yelled Ngozi. "Evac is coming!"

"If they break the shield, I'll try fighting them off the best I can," said Uzoma.

"Hopefully it won't come to that."

Moses quivered as the shield was barely holding. The three remaining monk warriors struggled with Keno holding the shield. Moses hoped eventually he wouldn't be next, or his mother and brother. But with the shield being tampered in such a way, hope was fading. The shield was visibly dark red. Ashanti held him and Ramses tight. Ngozi and Uzoma stood beside them ready for another attack.

"Here, take my dagger," said Uzoma to Ngozi. "You're going to need it."

Ngozi took the curved dagger from Uzoma while he unsheathed his sword.

The shield surrounding them hummed. The dark warriors stood in place. Amaryllis lifted one of her glowing hands causing the energy shield to shatter as it blew to dust. Moses gripped his mother trembling in her arms. He felt her patting his back while rubbing smoothly.

"It'll be okay," she whispered her voice crackling. "I promise."

Ashanti watched as the dark warriors took the advantage, replacing their lethal weapons with stun rays to incapacitate any person they encountered. People were screaming, scattering with efforts to either fight back or run. She could tell the rest of the men were not warriors, but farmers, masons, carpenters, businessmen trying to protect their families. However, they were no match for the dark warrior's skill in combat as they shocked them with stun rays.

Moses peered his eyes at the chaos surrounding him. Men were being harmed by stun rays causing them to separate from their families. Women were being separated from their children while being dragged to the ground. The children were placed in cuffs. There was nothing Ngozi, Uzoma, or the monks could do to protect them now. They were occupied with protecting the remaining members of the royal families. Keno and the monks surrounded Tulip and Kalia while slicing each dark warrior that drew laser swords at them.

Moses saw Ngozi charging at a dark warrior that stormed near them and slashed it with his dagger .and sword. Uzoma stood his ground in front of them, slashing dark warriors one by one instantly. He kicked one of them in the chest causing it to dive backward in Ngozi's direction as he stabbed it in the back. The dark warrior gurgled, laying flat. Ngozi turned to face Ashanti and her children.

"My lady, stay close to me," he said. "Me and Uzoma will get you out of here."

"How long until evac arrives?" she asked.

Instead of listening to Ngozi's response, Ashanti heard echoes of herself, *arrives? arrives? arrives? arrives?*

The world was spinning. She felt as if she was drowning losing the grip of her sons feeling darkness around her. Moses felt the same. It was as if he felt drugged. He didn't feel any pain, so he couldn't be dying. He saw his mother and brother in blank stares looking into the sky. Something was wrong. Before darkness had overtaken him, he saw Amaryllis smirking at him. Her eyes were malevolent. He gasped, hearing the echoes of it as he gazed at the dark clouds. All he could see was darkness, the sounds of turmoil erasing from his consciousness.

Moses' consciousness appeared inside the throne room. It felt like a dream. He wondered where his mother was. Where was his brother? Were they separated like the families he saw that suffered at the hands of dark warriors? Moses turned his head and saw them. They looked as baffled as he was with their eyes widened looking around the empty vast room. *Am I dead?* he thought. Moses patted his mother's hip to see if she was real. She looked down and patted Moses on his head, then turned and did the same to Ramses.

"Oh my," she said.

"Momma, is that really you?" asked Moses.

She looked as if she was amazed looking around the room.

"Yes my sweet, it's me."

"Where are we? Are we dead?"

She was silent. Her jaws were dropped while she stared at her hands. She looked at Moses, then turned to face Ramses. He was silent as well as confused. She turned back to Moses.

"No, I don't think we are dead. We are not dreaming either."

She glanced and saw the battle between her husband and the Shadow Lord letting out a gasp that inhaled a deep breath.

"This is a spell," she whispered.

"Fatha!" yelled Moses.

He could see the battle as well. Moses ran towards his father until his mother grabbed him from behind.

"No Moses!" she yelled. "Your father can not see nor hear you."

"But why? I'm right here."

"We are not physically here. That shadow witch must've put a hex on us."

"I don't understand."

"That means we're still outside, but our minds are trapped in here."

"But why would they put us here instead of trying to kill us out there?" questioned Ramses.

"I don't know" Ashanti responded. "But by the looks of things, we were sent here to look at the fate of this battle. I just hope you can defeat him, my husband. You can't hear me but please be strong Oba. Your kingdom is depending on you."

The Chieftain and the Shadow Lord paused for a moment, staring unto each other. Khonshu sensed the Chieftain's energy lowering from fatigue, it was soon time. The Chieftain felt out his enemy.

Something wasn't right. The Shadow Lord was barely out of breath. It was as if he was holding back.

Khonshu threw a jab to the Chieftain's face but was deflected. He threw more jabs, but the Chieftain held his ground. The Shadow Lord attempted a sweep kick, but the Chieftain dodged it shifting his body to the opposite direction from where he was standing. The Shadow Lord spun following suit, then got back into his fighting stance. The two were face to face anticipating each other's next move. But who would deliver the next blow? Khonshu decided to test his opponent's defense attacking the Chieftain with swiftness faking a jab then throwing a high kick. He was able to read the Shadow Lord's move and ducked. The Chieftain saw an opening and kicked him on the chest creating an echo that roared a thundering sound. Khonshu went flying across the room landing on his back as he crawled back to the stairs. His rib cage had to be cracked. Victory was within his grasp. The nightmare was coming to a close.

Moses cheered alongside his mother and brother giving each other high fives and hugs.

"You did it, my love," said Ashanti. "Now end this."

"You did it fatha," Moses whispered. "You did it."

The Chieftain walked towards Khonshu having him cornered with nowhere to run. Sparks shot out of the wounded area near his rib cage. He wheezed through his iron mask gasping for air.

"This ends now!" yelled the Chieftain. "Your reign of terror is finished!"

The Shadow Lord laughed instead of pleading for his life. He held himself, spitting out blood through his mask. The Chieftain was puzzled at the Shadow Lord's reaction to his defeat.

"Well done Chieftain Oba," Khonshu said. "I'll have to admit you were a worthy foe. I haven't faced off with somebody that strong in a long time. It's just too bad I have to kill you so soon."

"Stop bluffing you bastard! You are defeated! I will be the one to end you!"

Chieftain Oba looked at the throne. The traditional chieftain spear was standing next to it. This was his go to weapon to finish off his foe.

"I'm afraid I'm not," said Khonshu. You see I barely used two-thirds of my power against you. You only wounded me because I held back. Let me give you a demonstration."

The Shadow Lord stretched his hand forming a red energy ball with black sparks surrounding it. He took his other hand and placed it on the wound healing it instantly. He shot the energy ball at the Chieftain as his family watched horrified. Moses was nearly breathless as his father caught it, struggling to deflect it. He was driven backward due to the power the energy ball had. Khonshu's eyes glowed red as the energy ball disintegrated. Chieftain Oba fell, rolling backward.

"No!" shrieked Ashanti. "Oba, get up!"

Smoke was steaming from the Chieftain's body as he lied still. The tide of the battle turned as Khonshu gained back his strength standing tall. The Chieftain struggled to stand to his feet. His breathing was rapid, his energy was burning out. Khonshu grabbed him by the throat, lifting him with ease. The Chieftain gathered the rest of his energy and strength to break free from the Shadow Lord's grip, but it wasn't enough. The Chieftain could feel the Shadow Lord's power level rising as the grip of the choke was tightening. It was hopeless. His effort was now being taunted by an

enemy who purposely held back just to be entertained. His vision was blurred. He felt his breath being
cut, his arms dropped to his waist. Khonshu saw the
presence of the Chieftain's family through Amaryllis'
spell. He sneered through his mask at their pleads
and cries. Khonshu pulled the Chieftain closer to him
and spoke in a low tone, "Long live the chief."

Moses watched as the Shadow Lord crushed his
father's throat, ending his reign as he fell on the palace floor. His body was stiff as he exhaled a long
breath. His eyes rolled. Moses was beyond grief. It
was an understatement. The world seemed to spin
around him despite the spell he was in.

"No...!" was the long shriek his mother cried out.
She fell on her knees as Ramses cried beside her in
disbelief. Moses didn't know what to feel. It couldn't
be true. His father could not be defeated, not like
this. Moses stared at the empty vessel of his father,
then at the Shadow Lord. He could tell the Shadow
Lord mocked his death as he placed his foot on the
first step with satisfactory, a bittersweet victory as he
stared at the chieftain's spear. Rage started to boil inside Moses. His fists were pumped. He gritted his
teeth while clenching his jaw. Moses felt an emotion

he never thought was inside of him. He screeched which let out an echo in the room. The Shadow Lord was attentive as the boy stormed towards him.

"Moses!" cried out Ashanti reaching out to him. She felt hopeless watching her son step boldly to Khonshu.

Moses' ears were shut, focusing on his father's murderer. His shriek was deafening. Khonshu's eyes were widened experiencing a power greater than that of his opponent. The room was in a massive quake matching his voice. Moses' body glowed in a golden light as flares and sparks of lightning surrounded his small body. Khonshu took a step back staring at his defining power.

"You," he whispered. "It's you."

The power Moses felt evaporated as he took a swing at Khonshu. His tears dropped on the floor mixing it with his father's tears. Khonshu's eyes glowed red. Darkness surrounded Moses once again, then there was light. He found himself back in his physical presence alongside his brother and mother. The battlefield was emptying. The dark warriors were making quick work of capturing their prey. The warriors were barely holding their ground. Moses saw the remaining two monks lying in their pool of blood. He saw Ngozi appearing before his mother lending his hand.

"My lady is everything okay?" he asked.

Her wailing continued. Ngozi wept while placing her head on his shoulder. Moses hoped what he witnessed in the palace wasn't true. Ngozi embraced her feeling disheartened.

"I know," he said. "I felt it too. I'm sorry."

A dark warrior appeared behind them raising it's laser launcher aiming it at Ashanti's head.

"Watch out!" cried out Moses and Ramses as they turned to face the enemy.

Ngozi turned with a quick reaction and saw the laser getting ready to be unleashed. His hand glowed transferring his power to the dagger. He swiped the dagger at the dark warrior, his power unleashing forming a sharp ray of golden energy. The energy slashed the warrior in half through its stomach forcing the laser to miss her, instead shooting on the ground next to her. Ngozi looked down and saw Ashanti place a hand on the hilt of an energy sword beside a dark warrior's corpse and let out a battle cry getting to her feet. She kicked off her heels and stormed at the dark warriors slashing them one by one. Ngozi joined her while Moses and Ramses followed closely. They were united with Uzoma standing beside each other forming a circle, swords were drawn. Moses and Ramses stood in the middle, watching their last stand.

Mercius and Amaryllis watched in disbelief uncertain of how they would kill the remaining royal family of Nubariah.

"Go after them," Mercius commanded to his warriors. "I want them taken out immediately!"

Moses saw the group of dark warriors charging towards them. The dark warriors encountered them clashing swords. Ngozi, Uzoma, and Ashanti stood their ground slaying their enemies in unison. The dark warriors were like a flood gate. After rounding up the people in electric chains, ropes, and collars, they focused their attention on the warriors. Keno joined Ngozi and the rest. Kalia and Tulip were on his hip. Moses peeked at Tulip, their troubled eyes meeting. It was as if they were sharing their despair.

"I'm creating a portal now!" called out Keno to Ngozi and Uzoma. "This is our only escape!"

The Monk Master bent his knees, forming a sky-blue circle that opened a portal to another part of Shieria. Within the portal were palm trees with crystal blue water and a sandy beach. Behind them was a group of colorful beach houses. This was a paradise Moses was hoping to soon enter.

"Master Ngozi," said Keno. "It's now or never. The dark warriors are approaching. There is no hope. We did all we could, but they have outmatched us. I have set a portal to take us to Genies Island. There we can recuperate."

Ngozi shook his head. The thought of abandoning Nubariah only brought him grief. He failed at this point to protect his people in Palasera, perhaps all of Ouidah. But it was no excuse to abandon the other regions around the nation.

"I can't do this Master Keno," he said. "I have a sworn duty as a watchman to protect Nubariah, and I will carry it out till the death of me."

Keno nodded his head with approval and extended his arm.

"Then may the Supreme lookout for you."

Ngozi nodded grabbing the monk's arm feeling his arm being gripped with an agreement of making it out of this battle.

"Until we meet again," were the words they exchanged.

Keno stood side by side with the girls. Moses waved at them with sorrows. Kalia held on to Keno without looking back. Tulip turned and waved at Moses, the Monk Master dragging her along. Keno stood guard at the portal escorting the girls. Kalia was the first to enter the portal. The Monk Master stood guard after she entered. Tulip not too far behind closing in on the portal. Moses peered in horror at the dark warriors closing in. Ngozi, Uzoma, and his mother were in defense. Tulip was a few steps away from reaching the portal, Keno stalked the dark warriors with caution.

"Now," said Mercius.

Amaryllis released a ball of fire mixed with ash forcing the Monk Master to leap out of harm's way as a few captives behind him were turned into stone from the impact. Mercius focused his power on Tulip levitating her in midair.

"Tulip!" cried Keno.

He darted at the Shadow Lord and Goddess unsheathing his electro spear. Mercius waved his arm, forcing Keno into the portal shutting it behind him. Amaryllis created a portal that sucked Tulip in. Moses watched in dismay, hearing her scream. Then silence.

Uzoma gazed at the two Shadow Lords then focused his attention on the Chieftain's family. He got Ngozi's attention. The dark warriors were stalking them on their approach.

"Listen to me," said Uzoma. "Get the royal family out of here. I will deal with Shadow Lord Mercius."

"But Uzoma you are not strong enough to take him head-on," said Ngozi. "If we can stall them for just a second with a flashbang, then we will have our escape."

Uzoma shook his head.

"You are the watchman. I am only a foot soldier whose men died effortlessly at the hands of our enemies. I will only slow you down if I accompany you all. At this point, my life doesn't matter."

"But Uzoma too many lives have been lost today!" bawled Ashanti. "We can't afford to lose you too!"

"I'm sorry, but there's no time. The fate of Nubariah is in your hands now. Those boys you gave birth to are the future of this nation. You must go now. It was an honor serving you and your husband. Now go, I will distract them!"

Ngozi nodded his head and guided the royal family to safety down a path of one of the side entrances that led to a tunnel. Moses turned his head watching Uzoma for the last time. He saw the dark warriors closing in.

"Well, what are you fools waiting for? Go after them!" yelled Mercius at his warriors.

The dark warriors sprinted in unison going after them, their laser swords and launchers wielded. He felt his mother dragging him as they came near the tunnel.

"C'mon Moses," said his mother. "We need to move."

Ngozi gestured them to hurry down a flight of stairs that led to darkness. Moses was in a place of uncertainty but entering a dark place would be better than being the next victim of a laser sword and bullets. He fled down the steps into the dark tunnel alongside Ramses. Ngozi followed behind them.

While the others were fleeing to safety, Uzoma raised his hand as the dark warriors approached. A bright light flashed from his palm, blinding the dark warriors on the battlefield. A force of wind followed the flash, wiping away the dark warriors like an explosion.

Uzoma and Mercius locked eyes. The heavy impact didn't affect the Shadow Lord or his wife. Uzoma smirked, meeting the Shadow Lord's cold stare.

"I guess you have to go through me first," said Uzoma.

"Foolish," said Mercius. "I guess you are willing to die like the rest. The bold lone survivor."

"More like defend for my people, but I prefer honorable than bold."

The army of dark warriors surrounded Uzoma in readiness for the final blow. The Shadow Lord instead waved them off.

"Clear the area," Mercius said. "He's mine."

Uzoma grinned and dropped his sword. They were now in a stare-down as the captives screamed in agony.

Moses could feel their pain and suffrage, nearly weeping at the sounds of women and children wailing with the loss of freedom despite the dark tunnel he was walking in. Red lights flashed dimly within the concrete walls and bricked ground. Moses questioned his freedom. His kingdom was now gone. His father was brutally murdered. The family he once had was stolen from him. What was the point of escape? What was the point of anything? It was a silent walk of sobs as Ngozi led the way. Uzoma may have been a distraction, but to Moses, it seemed as if his sacrifice was already for nothing.

Chapter Five

Take Over

While Moses followed his family through the dark tunnel Uzoma stepped up to the Shadow Lord, fearless. Mercius stared at him emotionless not budging. The vast army of dark warriors circled the two monitoring the fight. The captives were in dread. Whatever hope they had of the clans saving them were now lost. Their freedom was gone. What Uzoma was doing to save them at this point was suicide, or at least they thought. Mercius let out a sneer opening his arms.

"Okay lion, your move," he said.

"With pleasure," said Uzoma.

He faked a right hook and threw a high kick to the temple of the Shadow Lord. He dodged the powerful kick while Uzoma slid on the pavement for a sweep kick. Mercius leaped from the attack and pressed his foot on Uzoma's head causing him to slide away. The Shadow Lord's speed was unimaginable. It was as if he was trying to touch a mirage.

Uzoma flipped to his feet getting back on his guard glaring at the Shadow Lord.

"Please tell me that's not all you got," said Mercius. "This fight is already boring me."

"I'm just getting started," said Uzoma.

Uzoma wiped his mouth and pumped his fists. He charged up his energy feeling electric static tingling from his stomach to the top of his head. Uzoma soared in midair gliding towards the Shadow Lord. Mercius used his unnatural quickness, backing away from Uzoma's multiple aerial kicks. He dropped to the ground with another attempt of a sweep kick. Mercius read his move and leaped away, soaring backward with his hands behind his back. Uzoma quickly got up to avoid another push to the head. He looked up, realizing the Shadow Lord was a few feet away. Uzoma gritted his teeth and darted at him. He threw a swift jab to the chest, but Mercius caught his fist and with a flash threw multiple punches on both jaws, chest, and stomach. Uzoma didn't see it coming. The Shadow Lord's fists were lightspeed. Uzoma lulled after the combos and was struck by an uppercut. Mercius walked up to the fallen warrior. Uzoma's mouth was drowned in blood as he lied with rapid breathing. The Shadow Lord planted his foot on his chest in a light press.

Uzoma's life force was fading, Ngozi could feel it. Moses could too as he followed his family out of the tunnel. His mother placed his head on the side of her hip humming him tunes while patting his head. There was no light at the end of the tunnel. The dark sky didn't allow it. The thought of predators in the wild made Moses nervous, but it was nothing compared to what he has been through. They were now at the end of the tunnel leading to a dirt trail with a grass plain beneath them of tall grass. It was dead silence as if the wild was sucked away. Moses was paranoid feeling the trauma of what took place hoping the dark warriors would not appear to them through their black magic. He could feel his heartbeat in rapid skips. His mother broke down in tears ending the silence that swarmed them. Ngozi placed his hand on her back.

"We have to move on your highness," Ngozi said. "When all this is over, I will give you the time to grieve."

"I know, it's just I don't know how to take all this in," she said. "My husband is gone. He's been taken from me and my children. Everyone else is gone. The palace has fallen..."

"Yes. We all witnessed it. But we must keep moving. The future of our nation depends on this moment."

She looked into his eyes with uncertainty. Ngozi saw Moses and Ramses hold on to her dress tight.

"You see those boys," he continued. "They do not need to see their mother like this. You need to stay strong for them. Remember, you are a lioness. They will grow up as lions and one day avenge our fallen. Do you understand?"

She nodded her head while wiping the tears from her eyes. Moses' fear turned to hope after hearing Ngozi's words. He looked at his brother, nodding his head. Ramses did the same. Although he was young, Moses could understand the importance of his family's survival. They were after all the heir of Nubariah, the very threat that could put an end to the Shadow League.

"Good," said Ngozi. "Now let's keep moving. We will be near the river soon."

Ngozi took Ashanti by the hand and strode through the trail leading to the grass plains. Moses grabbed his mother's hand and Ramses' following closely.

While Moses and his family continued their escape, Mercius threw another right hook to Uzoma's cheekbone while keeping his foot planted on his chest. Uzoma's face was stained in blood after receiving the torture the Shadow Lord was giving him.

"You are beaten general," Mercius said. "There is no hope for you. Tell me what I need to know, or I will finish you."

Uzoma grinned spitting out blood.

"Well why won't you then," he said. "Finish me off Shadow Lord, the task is done. You have failed. The royal family has escaped. The heir of Chieftain Oba will come back and destroy you."

The expression of impatience flashed through Mercius as he scowled at Uzoma.

"If you insist," he said.

The Shadow Lord balled his fist and lifted it. Uzoma closed his eyes, his life flashing. *It was an honor serving you my king*, he said in his head. He waited for the final blow so his suffering could end. At this moment he was ready to die, to face an honorable death. A few seconds passed and Uzoma felt nothing. He opened his eyes watching Shadow Lord Khonshu gripping Mercius' wrist, setting it down. Uzoma was in the realization that his death was delayed. How long would his suffering continue?

"That is enough Mercius," Khonshu said. "Torturing him is now pointless. We have everything we need."

"But the royal family of the Lion Clan," Mercius replied. "They still remain."

"Let them be. Hunting them will be a waste of time. They will run, but eventually, they will appear.

And the day they do we will finish them. For now, we have victory. Palasera has been sacked. All of Nubariah is ours for the taking."

"So be it."

Mercius released his foot from Uzoma's chest. He rolled to his stomach gasping for air with a string of blood gushing from his face. Uzoma slowly crawled away from the Shadow Lords, watching the captives sitting hopelessly on the palace grounds with electric ropes tied behind their backs and chains around their ankles. Collars were round on their necks. If only this pain would end. Uzoma felt the back of his shirt being gripped as he was dragged back to his feet.

"Don't think I was just going to let you go general," said Khonshu. "Now that we don't need you, I can just dispose of you."

Khonshu threw Uzoma in the air. The misery that engulfed him began to fade. Uzoma's life was receding, at least this point he hoped. Khonshu looked unto the sky at Uzoma's floating body. He opened his palm as glowing dark red energy ignited. The Shadow Lord unleashed the energy ball in the air sending it soaring to the Lion Clan General. Uzoma smirked, watching the red light as the energy ball dragged him away.

Moses continued to follow Ngozi and his family in the open grass plain. He knew that they were close. He could smell the scent of the river from a mile away. He heard the distant sounds of elepotoms resembling the sound of trumpets with monkeys screeching in packs. Then a familiar voice hollered with echoes from the air. His scream was of horror, the sound of torture through a thundering echo. Moses could sense the man's pain, Uzoma. Ngozi paused, gasping. Moses paused along with everyone else, looking at the grey sky. Uzoma was floating in pain, the energy ball carrying him through its radiant light. Then he disappeared.

"Uzoma," said Ngozi. "Looks like the Shadow Lord got him too. We can't let his sacrifice be for nothing. Let's keep moving."

"*Mast...*" sounded a voice on his Optix.

Ngozi grabbed the cube from his pants pocket. A man dressed in a white sailor suit with a white hat appeared through the holo-projector.

"Repeat," Ngozi said.

"Master Ngozi," said the man.

"I'm here."

"We have a problem."

"What is it? Because apparently, you're too late. The royal families are dead, and all the nobles are captured. The only survivors I managed to get out of there is Chieftain Oba's family. Even he didn't make it. Now, what the hell happened to you all? I called for evac twenty minutes ago!"

"My apologies for the delay but we have a bigger problem," said the man. *"Our systems are jammed. We sent the pods as you requested, but they had shut down and crashed mysteriously. Every single one of them."*

"Damn. They even used their magic to disrupt our systems. Abort the mission now. Do not risk sending any more pods out into the city. I won't allow you to lose your life on a suicide mission. Send a motorboat to the Lagun River. I will track you our location."

"I will send it immediately and we will abort on your command."

"Thank you, evac team."

Ngozi placed his Optix back in his pocket gesturing the royal family to move forward. Moses watched as a herd of elepotoms appeared from out of the trees into the trail. Their long body of ten feet quaked the ground. This was the signal for escape. There was no time to hesitate. Ngozi led the way following the elepotoms. A family of monkeys swung from the treetops following the elepotoms in loud chants blending in with the horn sounds the elepotoms were making. Moses was amazed by the abilities the animals had of leading them to the river. Moses followed Ngozi's lead, reaching the end of the trail. Moses clenched onto his mother's hand. Ramses held her other hand. They paced forward, following Ngozi behind the herd. The monkeys swung from the trees with the sound of water streaming along a bank. The trail has ended. The river was flowing before them, they finally made it. Moses was beyond relieved. From a distance, he saw a motorboat speeding towards them.

"Look," he said pointing at it.

"Just in time," said Ngozi. "Come, our ride is here."

The motorboat slowed down once it approached them, coming to an abrupt stop. There were two men in the boat. One was in the driver's seat. The other was on the ramp, the man in the Optix. Moses could recognize his face. The man got out of the boat to meet with Ngozi, bowing to him and Ashanti.

"Master Ngozi," the man said. "We came as soon as we could."

"You came just in time," said Ngozi. "We better leave immediately before those devils spot us."

The man assisted Moses, his mother, and his brother to the boat. They went inside the boat, Ngozi and the man following suit. The boat sped down the river after the man's command. Ashanti held Moses and Ramses in her arms, the boat speeding down the river for their escape out of the city. Moses was in sorrow. The thought of his father's death left a gaping wound that would not heal. Watching his home being destroyed by the Shadow League made him feel like an alien. It's like he lost himself, his identity. The innocence he once had was degraded. There was silence again. Ngozi wrapped his arms around Moses and his family in comfort.

While Moses and his family escaped from the carnage, the Shadow Lords stood triumphant in their conquest. Bodies of the warriors were all over the palace grounds as the people were maimed in shackles and collars. Khonshu gave the dark warriors the order to take the captives away while gathering the bloody corpses in a pile to burn.

"The Jaguar Clan has escaped before this encounter," said Mercius.

"Patience Lord Mercius," said Khonshu. "They will be dealt with. For now, let us bask in the victory of today. All the royal families are dead. And as long as Chieftain Oba is gone, the Lion Clan is powerless. Amaryllis, you said you had a surprise for me."

The Shadow Goddess smirked while sauntering to him.

"As a matter of fact, I do Lord Khonshu," she said. "The Monk King that you killed earlier had two daughters."

"Tell me what I don't know Amaryllis."

She rolled her eyes.

"I was just getting to the point my lord," she said. "The remaining Lion Clan leaders teamed up with monks while protecting them and Oba's family.

Unfortunately, one had escaped with I believe the monk leader. But I managed to capture this little one myself with my dark magic. Bring her to us."

A dark warrior grabbed Tulip from a portal below. She was in fright with tears welling. Khonshu stared at her for a moment, then nodded to the dark warrior to let her go.

"Come to me child," he said.

Tulip was hesitant, shivering instead of taking steps forward.

"Do not worry. I won't hurt you I promise."

Tulip walked towards the Shadow Lord, her legs twitchy. She gushed more tears feeling her body quiver almost losing balance. Mercius scowled while taking a few steps back to clear the way. Tulip approached Khonshu. Her head was down with her pulse feeling like sprints. She crossed her legs while rubbing her arm. Khonshu knelt to lock eyes on the girl. She squealed taking a step back. Her breathing was heavy after peering at his lava-colored eyes.

"It is alright," said the Shadow Lord. "I am Lord Khonshu. What is your name?"

She was timid, responding in hesitance, "T... Tulip."

"Tulip, what a lovely name. Tell me, Tulip, are you a princess?"

The girl slowly nodded.

"Yes, I know. You will make an excellent ruler when you grow up. And by my side, you will live that dream."

A huge outcry erupted from the direction of the palace. Khonshu rose back to his feet. He wondered how this could be. The last he checked every warrior and guard was dead. He sensed a familiar foe and clenched his fists. Tulip's eyes widened with joy. She could feel the live presence of her father.

Mongrel leaped from out of the palace brutalizing each dark warrior that stood in his way. Blood with the mixture of saliva hung from his mouth. Mongrel smashed two of the dark warrior's heads together while throwing massive swings to sweep them away like a tsunami. He spotted Khonshu with his daughter and leaped in midair towards them while charging his power.

"Tulip get out the way!" he yelled.

The little girl whisked away as Mongrel threw a colossal punch to Khonshu's skull hoping he would knock his head off his body. Instead, Khonshu blocked it, matching his power with Mongrel's. The impact left a crater on the pavement. Khonshu charged his power and front kicked Mongrel. Before Mongrel landed on his feet, Khonshu used his shadow energy to lift him only using his arm to guide the floating body. Mongrel struggled to break loose. He tried using a meditation technique of the monks but the spiritual energy he had was powerless against the Shadow Lord. Khonshu squeezed his fingertips to tighten Mongrel's arms from within his bloodstream. He grunted, his arms feeling like it's in a furnace.

"I am impressed that you have survived," he said. "You will make an excellent king within my empire. Just think of the power you will possess. You would become far more powerful, far wealthier. You will still be able to rule over your people under my subjugation. You may have lost your wife, but you still have your daughters. All you have to do is bow down before me."

Khonshu released Mongrel from his grip as he fell on his hands and knees breathing rapidly. He watched from the distance of his daughter trembling. Mongrel saw from the distance the bodies that were being piled together. One of the corpses was his wife. He looked for his other daughter to see if she was safe. However, she was nowhere to be found. He let out a roaring laugh, echoing the atmosphere. He tried to hold back the pain. Perhaps he wished death wouldn't elude him.

"You killed my wife," he said. "You destroyed my family. You might as well kill me too because I will never join you."

Khonshu glared into Mongrel's eyes then burst into laughter.

"Kill you?" he said mocking him in laughter. "I have no reason to kill you."

Khonshu's lips crinkled with his eyebrows furrowed. He gripped his fingers on Mongrel's cheeks staring into his flashing brown eyes.

"I will enjoy myself more watching you suffer," the Shadow Lord said. "Besides, I've already killed you. Now I will make you rot. First by taking your daughter making her my heir to replace you. Then I will take your kingdom. I will drain you to the point where your spirit will be destroyed. Then you will die. You should have joined me, monk. But I see you have made your choice. So now…"

Khonshu threw his elbow on the temple of Mongrel. The former Genies King collapsed on the pavement.

"Get the monk out of my sight," he said to one of the dark warriors. "I don't care if you drag him to the wild."

The dark warrior responded dragging Mongrel's massive body into a portal with the help of three others. Khonshu turned his attention to Mercius and Amaryllis. They stood side by side, their arms locking in unison.

"And now for the future of Nubariah," Khonshu said. "Now we have complete control of the clans with the fall of the Lions. The people of Nubariah are now subject to us. There will be little resistance. Now I must take care of another task. I will take an army with me to the North Pacific to ensure the Tiger and Dragon Clans won't try to rise against us. Although we've taken out the most sacred tribe in the world, we still must put the Outer Nations in check before a rebellion starts."

"They will fall just like the others," said Mercius. "Now what was your promise for us since we aided you in this conquest?"

Khonshu turned, facing the couple.

"I understand that you and Amaryllis will have a child soon."

Khonshu signaled one of the dark warriors to come forth from the palace entrance. The dark warrior had in its hand the Chieftain's traditional spear. Khonshu took the spear from the dark warrior and placed in in Mercius' hands.

"My gift to you is the entire nation of Nubariah. You will have full control and will be able to set any laws you see fit to establish your rulership."

The couple looked at each other in astonishment then back at the Shadow Lord.

"Why thank you Lord Khonshu," said Mercius. "Amaryllis and I are flattered."

"There is much that still must be done but the world will belong fully to the shadows," Khonshu said. "And the Shadow League will become the highest power of the Shadow Legion

He turned to Tulip motioning her with his finger to come. The little girl was stiff, hesitant. She feared the Shadow Lord more than the feeling of hatred. His power was too terrifying for her to defy him. The pride Tulip had for her people and native land was gone. She now felt empty with fear of her new guardian. She joined the Shadow Lord walking with him side by side to the army of dark warriors. They were around the captives, dragging each of them to their feet.

"Anyone that is of the Genies People send them to me and my new protégé," said Khonshu. "I want half of you to come with me to Genies Island. There we will subjugate the island. Soon after we will prepare our attack on the Dragon and Tiger Clans. The rest of you will report to Shadow Lord Mercius and Amaryllis for the rest of their conquest here in Nubariah. Take the rest of the captives in the palace. I'll let Lord Mercius decide what to do with them."

"Yes my lord," said one of the dark warriors.

The army of dark warriors bowed in unison to the Shadow Lord. They gathered the captives, forcing them to stand to their feet. The Shadow Lord stepped to the fearful crowd. He could see the terror on their faces with signs of hopelessness. Tulip was by his side watching in the sorrow of their suffrage. She only wished she had the courage and strength to help them.

"Whoever is a Geniesian step forth now," the Shadow Lord said.

A handful of people stepped up who were men, women, and children. The electric chains around them were sparking. Khonshu nodded his head, gesturing one of the warriors to ignite a portal.

"Princess," said one of the male captives.

Tulip turned and saw a man of a fit physique with salt and pepper colored hair trying to plea with her in his native Creole tongue.

"Mi know yuh young and ave fear, but yuh a chosen. Wen yuh grow up, yuh will ave strength like fi yuh fada, de king. Yuh mus tek bak de kingdom. You mus..."

Khonshu turned around facing the man, using his power to stiffen his entire body in a paralysis. Tulip turned her head to the ground while the man grunted, barely letting out a breath. The chains were dangling from his wrist and ankles

"I see already I need to set an example," said Khonshu.

He waved his arms, forcing the man to turn to face the captives. Khonshu used his power to force the man's body to levitate. Tulip could hear his cries. She could feel his suffrage. The crowd gasped with shrieks of horror witnessing Khonshu's terrifying power.

"Since you want to have a conversation let's talk," said Khonshu. "Let's all talk."

He circled the man stalking his every feature.

"You seem strong," said the Shadow Lord. "You would be an excellent builder. I see the potential. But your defiance will cost you. Now tell me, what is your name?"

The man groaned with the inability to make out a sentence. Tulip could tell he was in too much pain to speak.

"I asked you a question!" roared Khonshu.

The man's groan grew louder.

Tulip could hear women speaking in whispering voices through different dialects of Creole, "For heaven sake just tell him your name."

Khonshu waved his hand, forcing the dirt around the captives to explode from the ground. Tulip shrieked falling flat on her behind.

"I don't need any instigators!" bellowed Khonshu.

The Shadow Lord gripped the man's body tighter causing him to shriek. His echoes were unbearable to Tulip.

"Are you ready to talk now?" asked Khonshu.

"Okay... Okay," said the man. "My name is Keon."

"See, was that so hard? Now that we have introductions out of the way, how about you share to your fellow brethren what you have shared to my newfound protégé."

Keon was silent.

Khonshu scowled, causing Keon's spine to crack. He screeched with another echo vibrating the air.

"Go on tell them," the Shadow Lord said.

The crowd was startled. Tulip could tell because she felt the same. It was as if she could feel Keon's agony, his bones grinding his flesh.

"Go on!" roared Khonshu.

Tulip saw that Keon was beginning to fade. His eyes were weak with the shortness of breath. Khonshu humiliated him continuously, gripping his cheekbones while jerking him to the captives.

"Tell them what you said!"

Keon faded. His eyes were shut. His body was in a complete limp. Khonshu huffed, throwing Keon to the ground with his dark power. Keon lied motionless. The captives screamed in terror. Tulip covered her eyes wincing in stained tears. Khonshu stepped on the man's back glaring at the crowd. His stare was vicious. The captives held each other, their electric chains and shackles sparkling.

"So, who wants to go next?" Khonshu questioned.

The captives were silent.

Khonshu smirked through his mask gesturing to one of his warriors.

"Take this man's body and add it to the pile of corpses. What a waste."

The dark warrior obeyed Khonshu's demand, grabbing the man's fresh corpse and dragging him to the collection of slain bodies. Khonshu drew his attention to the captives.

"Take the rest of them to the portals," he said to the dark warriors.

The dark warriors responded dragging the Geniesian captives to the portal in silence. Khonshu stood with his arms folded beside his new protégé. Khonshu nodded his head to his remaining dark warriors. They dragged the rest of the captives to the palace waiting for further orders from Shadow Lord Mercius.

"When the time comes you will learn the Shadow Arts," said Khonshu to Tulip. "And you will learn true rulership. Now come with me, my new apprentice. It is time to introduce Genies Island's new ruler."

Khonshu walked side by side with Tulip. She looked around at the emptiness of the palace grounds. She mourned at the sky of what was a beautiful day. Her lamentation was of losing her family witnessing the death of her mother, her father being forced into the wilderness, the separation of her sister. She entered the palace as the princess of the Genies King and Queen, then made her exit out as the Shadow Lord's apprentice. They walked into the portal together, the sandy beaches awaiting them.

Outside of the palace grounds, the motorboat sped away from the presence of the Shadow Lords. It was silence in the atmosphere. Moses laid his head on his mother's lap next to Ramses. She sat still with many sorrows. Ngozi sat in front of Ashanti and her children.

"I can never understand your pain," he said. "But I am hurt as well. So are your sons. I've known Oba all my life. My heart truly breaks for you, your highness."

Without looking at him Ashanti responded, "You have no idea the feeling I have right now. Today I lost a husband. My sons lost a father. The kingdom that we've built, that our ancestors built from the hands of the Supreme is gone. It has been taken from us.

Now we are vulnerable with nowhere to go. Why has this happened to us? What will we do now Ngozi? Please tell me."

Ngozi stared at her.

"We are not vulnerable," he said. "I know a small village where the Shadow League will not be able to detect us. We will be safe there until our next course of action."

Tears gushed out of Ashanti. Moses could feel the pain too. The fresh thought of losing his father was unimaginable. If only this was a dream. He cried too alongside his mother and brother. Ngozi embraced the three in a group hug.

"Death is only a gateway to another life," he said. "You see those boys. Oba's spirit is with them. Things may seem grim now, but once your boys get older, Nubariah will have liberation. The Lion Clan will once again rise and take back the kingdom."

But she couldn't take his words to consideration, neither Moses nor Ramses. Not at a time like this. The feeling of grief to lose her husband and the father of her children was too much to bear. Moses was stiff, his head resting on his mother's lap. Ramses placed his head on her shoulder staring at the black clouds with grief. Ngozi did what he could to comfort the Chieftain's family. But he knew at this moment they needed time to grieve. They were safe, at least for the moment. Ngozi stood to his feet, his focus on Ashanti.

"Be strong your highness," he said. "Your boys will take back what is lost. Soon a king will arise and Nubariah will be set free."

Subjugation

Oppression was at an all-time high for the Nubarian people as seven years passed by. After staking claim of Nubariah, Mercius renamed the nation the Bronze Empire and he became their emperor.

In Ouidah, people were constantly trafficked each day divided from their family and homes rather it was women or children. Wives were sent as concubines for foreign lords and countrymen who had money for trade in their self-pleasure. Men were no longer the women and children's protector as they would be executed daily if they were to try and practice kung dambe or get caught reading the scrolls of their ancestors. Everything belonging to Ouidah was stripped. The rations of food were very little. Children were left begging on every corner for food or water rather they were with their families or sheltered themselves. Thievery was now common in society as thugs who worked for the mercenary syndicates took over the streets of Palasera and other neighboring cities working as the Shadow Lord's eyes to make sure there were no potential rebels to go against the throne. They also helped with the trafficking of women and children rather they were married, widowed, or a maiden.

The prominent social class of Ouidah diminished. The nobles that once served the High Chieftain within political affairs became personal servants of Mercius and Amaryllis, the new royal family of their empire. Native business owners lost their businesses to the wealthy families and merchants of the outer nations leaving them with nothing but scraps as they were left to work hard through slave labor along with the working class who were forced into free labor in exchange for housing.

After the death of Hullu, The Oph-Ur Clan of the Aswan Territory was watched over by Queen

Nadiyya, the niece of the deceased Chieftain. Mercius declared her as one of his proxy leaders for his empire. The Queen was given a deal by the Shadow Lord that the people of Aswan would be free from hard bondage as long as she would abide by his laws and institute reeducation camps as well as labs reserved mainly for eugenics. Queen Nadiyya had no choice but to comply or she would get assassinated and replaced with a leader of Mercius' choosing.

The Queen took matters into her own hands and built the underground city of New Ubana where people could live their lives freely separated from the Bronze Empire without having to worry about the Shadow Lord's treacherous laws and clinics. The women were able to birth as much children as intended with their husbands. The people were able to follow their culture freely that has been taught from generation to generation. New Ubana was the only city for such freedom, and the Shadow Lord had no idea of the city's existence.

Since his exile, King Mongrel was driven insane as he lived in a hut beside the shore within Genies Island after years of searching for his daughters. They were nowhere to be found. The villagers and towns people became servants and hustlers under the rulership of Khonshu and kings within the outer nations. The monks were all but powerless against the Shadow Lord's power as they were forced into hiding above the underbrush of the forest. Without the monk's protection and the King's leadership, gangs began to take over the streets within the towns of the island which the leaders reported to the Shadow Lord.

Princess Kalia trained under Master Keno within the Monk Clan nearly becoming as strong as her father. Since the death of her mother and believing her father was dead, she lived with the monks in their hidden enclave away from the Shadow Lord moving up the ranks to become one of the top warriors within the clan. Her younger sister Tulip trained in the dark arts under Shadow Lord Khonshu himself. She hasn't seen her father since the Shadow League's attack. Her sister was far from her reach. There was no hope for her, only fear. In her heart, she knew she wasn't evil, but she felt she had no choice but to consume the darkness. Her young years were full of darkness, a nightmare she couldn't wake up from. She witnessed the change of the island. She witnessed foreigners taking over the wealthy class that once supported her father's rulership. She witnessed how her people were left with scraps, had to hustle by selling tourists handcrafted merchandise. She witnessed the servants working long hours to make ends meet rather they served the wealthy families or merchants. All hope was lost for the young princess. She became a part of the shadows looking for a beacon of light.

Within Mombassa, Chieftain Thuku continued to lead his people in exchange of complying to the laws of the Bronze Empire honoring the Shadow League's symbol and image. There were no foreigners within the territory that has taken over any class within Thuku's government. However, the freedoms the Chieftain's people had were at a cost.

The people were reeducated to put their customs and beliefs in the backburners of their thoughts in exchange for the customs of the outer nations. Families were controlled and governed by the Shadow Lord's policies as every married couple within the territory would only be limited of birthing two children per household. If any man or woman would birth an extra child and get caught, the parents would get executed and the children would be sold to the outer nations. Citizens from infants to the elderly were required to take injections from clinics or they would be arrested and executed.

Mercius declared the Bronze Empire as a nation of foreign shopkeepers and merchants, with tourism and trade of goods. With all hope lost, the natives who were once prosperous, became a people of thieves and tricksters, living life through desperation and oppression. Palasera itself came from the Golden City of the Lion Clan to the Great City of Emperor Mercius. Nubariah was in complete darkness with Sahawayda being the only land in Shiveria that had its light.

Chapter Seven

Painful Memories

*M*oses… was the sound of a whispering voice. It was a familiar sound. Moses found himself appearing from a cloud of smoke in the form of his younger self. He stared at his arms. He looked at his feet. The kaftan he was wearing looked similar. Was he four years old again reliving that fatal moment?

"No, not again," he whispered to himself.

Moses my son, come to me.

"This isn't real," he said closing his eyes. "This isn't real."

Moses.

The voice was closer. Moses could feel the voice's breath touching his face. He opened his eyes. His father was standing in front of him. The throne appeared behind them. The empty space morphed into the throne room through a puff of smoke. Moses welled in tears placing his head on his leg. His father smiled wrapping his arm around him.

"It's okay son. I'm here."

"Fatha please watch out for him this time," said Moses.

"Watch out for who son?"

"That evil man."

Moses looked up watching his father's smile.

"It's okay son. I promise nothing will happen. I will protect you."

Behind his father, Moses saw another cloud of smoke appearing in the form of a monstrous beast. It had the skin of ash with tendrils of smoke around its body. The beast had bulky features and its eyes were red with teeth sharp as iron. The look of the monster was all too familiar.

Moses could hear his heart beating out. He backed away pointing at the creature.

"Fatha, watch out!"

His father turned around, but it was too late. The beast wrapped its fingers around his throat. That moment once again was relived. Moses screamed watching his father lose his breath once again. His long-winded gasp echoed the air. The beast growled then turned back to Moses in a smirk.

"You're next," it said letting out a roar.

Moses gasped and found himself on his bed holding his neck. It was another nightmare. He was back in the reality of his new home Dolsa, the flyspeck of a village ran only by water panels for electricity near a grassy plain by a river full of wildlife roaming free. He looked at his arms. Then he got out of the bed and stared at his feet. His body was back in his eleven-year-old form.

It has been seven years since that fatal day which changed Shiveria by storm. This was a change Moses had to endeavor in his own life. He came from a home of royalty in Palasera to a common single-parent home in Dolsa.

Moses walked towards the window to open the blinds. The moon still shined in the night sky. He couldn't go back to sleep. There was no comfort for him at home to talk about this recurring dream. His mother always told him that is part of the trauma they are all dealing with. Ramses would possibly tell him how much of a punk he was for being so scared. Moses slipped on a pair of black striped cotton wrap pants with a grey shirt. He figured his mother was in a heavy sleep. A royal always gets the best sleep. Moses slipped on a pair of sandals and opened the window. He climbed out and shut the window behind him leaving a small crack.

Moses walked about on the dirt road hoping to clear his thoughts. He sought answers to why the memory of his father's death haunted him in recurring dreams from Ngozi and the other masters. Each answer he got was "let go of your personal feelings, meditate day and night". Moses was forever in gratitude to Ngozi leading the escape from Palasera to Dolsa. It became known as the Thousand-Mile Voiceless Journey.

Moses caught himself sitting on a wooden market stand of ripe plantains sitting on rows of baskets. He stared across from him at a stand of empty baskets where powdery sugar doughnuts and coconut chocolate chip cookies were sold. Moses knew that his vile mentality was getting the best of him. Usually, his cravings were for those sweet delicacies that would leave a satisfying taste in his mouth. His mouth usually waters with the soft and warm chewy tastes of doughnuts before venturing the academy in the morning. He would save the cookies for later. But even those treats couldn't make him happy nor get over the pain.

It was only a few hours until the markets would be open for business. Vendors were preparing the stands for their daily sales. This was the best time to go out for a walk before the village would get busy. Moses let out a deep sigh and stared at the moon once again.

"Moses," said a young boy around the same age as him.

He turned around and gasped after returning from his inner dark thoughts. His best friend Korah appeared from the market stand behind him.

"Korah? What are you doing here? Wait, as a matter of fact, what are you up to now?"

"It's funny you should ask. I'm just practicing my technique before training today. Then I saw you. Now, what are you doing here? Shouldn't you get any beauty sleep before the academy?"

"Korah, you don't understand."

"Oh c'mon Moses. Don't give me that madness of how sad you are. You need to lighten up. Loosen up a bit."

"I'm not in the mood Korah. I just went outside to get some fresh air. I keep getting these nightmares about…"

Moses paused stooping his head and cuffed his face in his hands. He held back his tears. Korah sighed and grabbed a chair made of straw from a stand next to them of yams. A man wearing glasses at the stand of yams stared at him with suspicion. Korah pulled the chair next to Moses for a seat.

"Moses, do you know how made you have it compared to the rest of us in training? You are being personally trained by Grand Master Ngozi to learn Kung Dambe. I mean Ramses is too, but still, you have an advantage. Why can't you just ask Master Ngozi? He has the answer for everything."

"It is not that simple," he replied. "Since I was five years old, I was told to put my sorrows aside. Master Ngozi gave me and my brother little time to grieve. He wouldn't even allow me to cleave to my mother. Master Ngozi gave me a choice to either toughen up or perish from training. Yes, I did come a long way since my first day of training. But I haven't recovered from the trauma."

Korah rolled his eyes.

"I didn't come all this way to hear your sad stories."

He paused with a mischievous smile.

"I know how to lighten the mood."

Moses sighed.

"What is it this time Korah? You don't seem to get it don't you?"

"I'm going to find you a wife."

Moses gasped nearly losing his breath. *He has to be kidding me*, were the thoughts on his mind. Only Korah would think of something foolish.

"This is a joke, right? You know I am far too young for that kind of stuff. Girls are the least on my mind."

Korah shrugged his shoulders.

"Well, I guess you'll have to miss out. I do know a perfect match for you. And she would love to be a future wife of the Chieftain's son. But I'll just leave you in your thoughts."

Korah walked away.

"Wait," said Moses.

Korah turned around grabbing one of the plantains.

"Hey boy, I hope you are planning to pay for those," said the man at the nearby stand.

Korah smiled innocently and placed the plantain back in the basket.

"Korah? Who is the girl you are talking about?" questioned Moses.

"It's a surprise."

Moses got up from the stand.

"Fine but make it quick."

Korah grinned, patting Moses on his back.

"Now you are talking. Let's do this."

Moses followed Korah down the road. The road was empty. Only the elders were out and about tending to the fields with a few warriors practicing fighting techniques. There were only a few guards at a time patrolling the village. Moses was feeling uneasy. Not only because of his thoughts, but this rite of passage seemed to be bad timing. Moses once overheard Ramses talking to his friends about the process of marriage. He heard Ramses say something about marrying a young woman of Ouidah taking more than a year, possibly several. A man must ask for the young woman to be with him and make an agreement. Then he would have to negotiate the marriage plans through a middleman, test the bride's character, and pay what is called bridewealth. Moses was only a boy. But here he was looking for a future wife that he was too premature to handle. This was not making him feel better.

They stopped at a small house made of cement blocks. The house was tattered with a rusted iron roof. Palm trees and bushes surrounded the small landscape of dirt and dust. Korah and Moses walked towards a metal door that appeared past its prime.

"Now you let me do the talking," said Korah. "I'm the expert in women."

"Have you even had a girlfriend?" wondered Moses.

"C'mon, what kind of question is that?"

Korah gave the door five knocks and stepped back.

"Don't you think everybody is sleep?" wondered Moses. "Let's go back, this is stupid."

"Don't be such a chicken," said Korah walking back to the door.

He banged on the door with loud thuds that echoed. Lights flickered on from within the house with sudden ramblings of a man letting out a swear. Moses' legs felt like it was in a block of ice. He wanted to run, but it was too late. The door opened revealing a tall brown man with a goatee. He was shirtless wearing silk green pajama pants and slippers. Moses wanted to gasp but couldn't, staring at the intimidating looks the man gave him. He had to be a warrior because of his muscular features. Or probably a guard.

"The hell is wrong with you knuckleheads?" he questioned. "You startled my wife and girls!"

"My... apologies sir," Korah stumbled over his words then cleared his throat. "I wanted to speak on behalf of my friend Moses. You know... the son of late Chieftain Oba. Out of respect, I wonder if he can... um... take your daughter Onyeka in the hands of marriage?"

The man looked at Moses and Korah in a blank stare.

"You're kidding me?" he said. "This is a joke right?"

"Uh, sir... he is the son of Oba..."

"I know who he is, and don't you have no shame boy for the ridiculousness you are pulling right now?"

The man stared at Moses. He wanted to defend himself, but he was in a shell shock. Moses was embarrassed. Out of all girls to pick an impossible marriage, Korah had to pick the girl who annoys him almost every day in the academy. He had to be out of his mind.

"I'm talking to you boy," said the man.

"But sir, you didn't ask my question about marriage," said Korah

"You know what, you two get the hell out of my property before I call the guards."

"But sir…"

"Out!"

The man slammed the door.

"C'mon Korah, let's go," said Moses.

"No, I'm not done yet," he smirked.

"Korah, enough of this…"

He cut his words off.

"Listen Moses. You're the son of Oba, so that means you're royalty. I said I was going to find you a future wife, and Onyeka is definitely the one. So you go towards the east and I'll go west. We will meet each other at the backyard."

Korah took off to the west side of the small yard before Moses could say another word.

"I'm regretting all of this," Moses said to himself.

He took off east. Moses was relieved there weren't any dogs barking nearby. He tiptoed at the side of the yard. So far, the coast was clear. All that surrounded him was chirping crickets with palm leaves waving in the calm breeze. Moses crept towards the back and saw Korah staring at a window made of wood far from the back door.

"This is her room," he whispered. He picked up a pebble and threw it at the window. *Tick,* was the sound the pebble made. No one answered. Korah sighed and threw multiple rocks that thudded the window. A girl with cornrows in a red shirt opened the window with rage.

"I'm trying to sleep!" she snapped. She looked down and saw Moses and Korah staring at her.

"Korah? Moses? What are you doing here?"

Her voice was now in a whisper.

"Onyeka, I need you to do me a favor," said Korah.

She sighed with her eyes rolled and folded her arms.

"What is it Korah?"

"Can you convince your father to take Moses' hand in marriage?"

Onyeka nearly choked.

"Eww no. Are you serious?"

"This is no joking matter. You don't have to agree to marry him now, but let it be for the future. My friend really needs a woman to make him feel good about himself. Besides, he is the son of Oba. And that means he will take the throne. Moses would shower you in precious rubies."

"Rubies huh."

Onyeka thought for a moment and cringed.

"I'm not doing such a thing. Plus, I never see Moses with anything valuable that a woman wants."

"C'mon please? Moses will get you what you need when we all get older."

Onyeka paused for a moment collecting her thoughts. She could tell by expression that Moses was feeling down. She almost felt for him. But the thoughts of marriage at the age of eleven were like committing suicide.

"I can't," she said. "Maybe one day Moses will be a good husband, but the thought of marriage sounds ridiculous. None of us has even reached puberty yet. Or at least I think."

"Don't tell me those boys still out there!" was the sound of the man in the background of the house.

"Yes, they are baba," said the voice of a little girl.

"You two need to go, now," said Onyeka.

Korah and Moses took off back to the front yard. The patted sounds of their feet resonated on the red dirt. The man opened the front door in rage.

"You damned kids, ya'll get back here or I'm going to call the guards!"

"Ignore him and keep running!" yelled Korah.

Moses did the exact. He did not look back hoping they wouldn't be chased down by an angry father. Moses ran down the road. He saw Korah sprinting next to him.

"Hey! Stop those two!" cried out the man.

Moses heard footsteps trailing in their direction. They were heavy boots with jingling keys. Only guards wore boots. Now he started to regret coming with Korah. Some friend he was getting him in trouble over some crazy rite of passage that he was too young for. His mother would kill him if she found out that he not only snuck out of the house but got into trouble. She was always overprotective of him and his brother since their father's death. If only he would have stuck with the fresh air.

"Hey, get back here!" said the guard from behind.

"It's a guard, split up!" yelled Korah.

Moses sprinted down the street hoping to lose sight of the guard. His arms and legs were pumping like a steam engine. He looked back and saw the guard coming after Korah. Although Korah caused this, Moses couldn't allow his friend to get caught. He was already frowned upon in the School of Combat. For once Moses had to take the blame. He yelled getting the guard's attention.

"Hey, lapdog! Over here!"

The guard turned and scowled. Korah's eyes were widened as Moses gestured for him to run. The guard was heated, Moses could tell as he chased after him. Moses heard heavy footsteps of boots pacing close behind him. Korah was on the clear.

"Stop boy or I will take you down!"

Moses fled with hopes of reaching back to the market square. His training was at least paying off. Both his stamina and agility increased over the years. It showed as Moses was outrunning the guard. Moses could hear the exhaling of his breath. Then the atmosphere around him felt as if it was still. This was a feeling Moses never felt. He stared at his arms and legs again. Moses felt normal but his surroundings froze. He was in a panic then gasped for air stopping in his tracks. Then a hand grabbed his shoulder from behind.

"You thought you could escape huh boy," said the guard.

He turned Moses around to face him. The guard had a scowl. Now he was in trouble. Moses had to face the punishment that awaited him.

"You knuckleheads are getting ridiculous. If you're not stealing from the markets, then you busy harassing villagers. Come here!"

The guard grabbed Moses while he was squirming for an escape.

"I know your mother boy. She would be ashamed seeing a potential heir stoop so low."

Moses stooped his head in anger. How dare he talk to him like that? Guard or not, Moses refused to feel disrespected. His bloodline was still of royalty rather he lived in rags or treasures.

"I should report you to your master. But instead, I will let you off with a warning. Is that understood?"

Moses glared.

"Is that understood boy?"

Moses nodded.

"Take it easy on him Ijendu," said Ramses from behind.

Ramses, now fourteen years old was twice the size as Moses. He was tall, cut with muscular features. His voice was as deep as a man's. He had on a hooded kaftan covering his ponytail locs. Moses wondered how his brother was able to find him.

"Ramses," said the guard. "It's a good thing you're here. I caught him and his friend at a house. The way they were running, they were either foolish enough to steal their possessions or they were trying to sneak to see a girl."

Ramses stared at a house next to them for a moment in thought then cackled.

"You have a lot to learn about women my little brother. I'll take it from here."

"Of course," said the guard. "I'm going to return to the house to make sure the brother and his family are okay."

He glowered unto Moses.

"You should follow your brother's example."

The guard walked away. Moses was left face to face with his brother. His fists were pumped. His jaws were clenched. Ramses laughed, patting his hand on Moses' wooly afro as if he was a dog.

"Lighten up brother, you seem so uptight," he said.

"How do you know I was out here?" questioned Moses.

"It's funny you ask. Mother sent me to find you. And here I find you into trouble."

Moses was in a shell shock.

"How do Mother know I was gone?"

Ramses smirked.

"Ask for yourself."

Moses gasped. His mother appeared in front of him with her arms crossed. She was in a skirt with a headscarf covering her hair. She glared at Moses with her lips pinched. He was officially in trouble.

Loyalty

M other, I'm sorry," said Moses.

His hands were clasped together. His eyes were in innocence. But his mother was in a constant scowl. Moses spotted Ramses smirking beside her. If only he could punch him in the stomach.

"I don't want to hear it," his mother said. "This is the second night in a row. What is wrong with you boy to be wondering about like this so?"

Moses thought of an excuse rather than admitting the truth of his internal pain. He didn't want to see her in grief.

"I just couldn't sleep, Mother."

"You are lucky that the patrols know who you are. But this will not give you an excuse of the punishment Master Ngozi will give you."

"But Mother..."

"But nothing. What is it that disturbs you so for you not to get any sleep? I can see why your performance has not been adequate recently in your studies and combat. I'm raising young men here. You should follow the example of your brother here instead of following up that Korah boy. He's going to get you in a lot of trouble."

Moses cracked his mouth open, but his mother prevented any sounds from coming out. Her glare was far more vicious than her previous look. It was as if Moses' chest was caved in. He was discouraged with his head stooped. Moses was silenced once again. His voice didn't matter at this point. It never did. It's as if his brother was glorified in the village as some kind of hero. But Moses could see through him. He could see through his broad shoulders and arms of brawn. Ramses grew to be a strong and cunning warrior, but Moses knew of his manipulation. He just had to prove it, or one day defeat him in one on one combat to expose his weakness. If it was only possible.

His mother had her finger pressed on Moses' lips.

"Not another word boy," she said. "Now come to the house right this instance. Maybe you'll get at least 30 minutes of sleep before starting the day of your studies and training."

Moses replied, "Yes Mother."

He followed her and Ramses down the road back to their house in an unpleasant walk. He wanted to tell his mother how much of a good friend Korah was to him. Out of everyone in the academy, including his brother, Korah was the only person who had Moses' back. It wasn't always like that. Moses was the least favorite since Ramses' popularity grew a few years ago and it wasn't because of his birthright alone. The more he shined the dimmer Moses became which he was soon forgotten. What kept him going over the years was Ngozi although he couldn't play favorites. Through Ngozi, Moses was encouraged to balance out his education and martial arts skills and become the best that he could be without distractions.

While following his mother and brother down the dirt road, Moses thought of Korah hoping that he was okay. Yes, Korah was a troublemaker. Moses couldn't deny it. The Council always thought Korah wasn't worthy to train as a warrior. But Moses helped him to better improve his fighting skills.

"They don't know nothing about him," he muttered to himself. "They weren't there."

Moses thought of the day he first met Korah and how since that day they stayed close.

***

It was four years ago on a hot summer day as Moses went up to the market stand of pastries. He had to get his mind off his brother and how the Council bragged about the might he had for his age. He could smell the sweet scent of fresh chocolate chip cookies. He was craving for the powder sugar doughnuts, but the cookies were calling his name as if it had a purpose. The lady behind the market stand smiled.

"Hello, what would you like today?"

Moses thought for a moment, the cookies or the doughnuts?

"I'll have the two cookies please," he said.

"That will be 3 nurubas."

Moses handed the woman three gold coins in exchange for the two oozing cookies of melted chocolate chips. Moses took his first bite. The chocolate chips were melting in his tongue with the sweet-soothing taste of the cookies. But his sensation ended as a boy the same age ran past him. The boy's clothes were frayed. His skin was ashy. The boy's hair looked like rolls of wild peas as if he didn't brush his hair in days. A group of boys sped past Moses on bicycles. One of them bumped into him, forcing him to drop his cookies on the ground. Moses' eyes were lit up. He could not escape having a problem with anyone in the village.

The boy slipped on the dirt and rolled to his stomach. He tried to get up but the boys on the bicycles circled him like vultures ready to devour their prey. Moses watched from afar. His jaws were opened wide. They're going to beat him up and nobody is going to break them up?

"We got him now," said one of the boys on the bike.

"Please, I'm sorry," the boy begged on his knees. "I won't do that again, I promise."

"Get him!"

The boys got off their bikes and ambushed the boy. They circled him with punches and kicks while everyone around the marketplace let out whispers. No one felt like breaking up this unfair beating. Moses was always taught that one on one combat was honorable, but a group against one person was an act of cowardice. If no one was going to help the boy, then Moses had to. He couldn't stand bullies, not even his big brother and friends. He acted fast before the damage would get worse. He stormed towards the boys and yelled, "Hey! Only cowards fight unfairly!"

One of the boys turned around as the others stopped in unison. He had to be the leader of the pact.

"The hell you said to me?" said the boy.

Moses stared at the boy's glare.

"Why won't you leave him alone and try that on me."

The boy walked up to him and smirked.

"This boy think he can take me. I guess I'll have to teach him a lesson too."

The boy wasted no time and hurled a right hook towards Moses' jaw. Moses watched the boy's long-arm curving towards his direction and blocked it with his back fist. He punched the boy on the side of his chin as he staggered back. Moses got into his fighting stance that Ngozi taught him to defend himself. He scanned the other boys. There were four of them.

Moses looked at the helpless boy peeking up with his nose bloodied and lips stained in a gash.

The boy held his chin in agony and scowled pointing at Moses.

"Get him!" he commanded the boys behind him.

Moses planted his foot seeing who he would take down first. They were looking to corner him, Moses read their movements. Moses grabbed one of them by the shirt and flung him on one of the other boys. They collided and fell on the dirt as Moses back fist a third boy on the jaw which impacted in a *cluck!* The fourth boy attempted to hook a punch at Moses, but he ducked and punched him on the stomach causing him to lose breath as he fell face first. Moses stepped up to the leader, fist clenched.

"I'm giving you a chance to run away," said Moses.

The boy looked over Moses' shoulder and called out, "What are you waiting for? Get him!"

Moses turned around and saw the two boys he flung to the ground getting up and ran to Moses with intentions to double team him. Moses ducked and tossed one of the boys to the ground using his back strength. He kicked the other boy in the face in a 180-degree turn. The leader attempted to punch him from behind, but Moses felt his presence and elbowed him on the chest with a *thud*! The boy gasped for air as Moses punched him multiple times in the ribs and jaws. The boy collapsed groaning in pain sounding like he was ready to cry. Moses let his guard down, the deed was done. Everyone around the market clapped as Moses smiled and took the helpless boy's hand.

"Are you okay?" Moses asked.

"I am now thank you," said the boy.

"I'll send you for aid."

The boy waved his hand.

"No, I don't want my mother to find out about this. If she does, she's going to kill me."

"What did you do?" wondered Moses.

"It's a lot to explain. But to make a long story short, they kept harassing me because my sister didn't like that boy back, and I paid them in return."

The boy flashed a tiled hat of multiple colors from his pocket. Moses flashed his eyes.

"So you stole from him?" Moses questioned.

"Not to take it, but I was going to prank them tomorrow by placing the hat in one of his friend's pockets. It would've been entertaining to watch them beat each other over something silly like a hat."

"But you got caught."

The boy placed his head down frowning.

"I just... I hate bullies. They all need to be taught a lesson."

"I hate them too," said Moses. "But do you know the best way to deal with them? My master said the best way to deal with an enemy is defense."

"You're from the School of Combat, aren't you? You guys train like every day."

"Want to join? I can give my master the word that you are interested."

The boy frowned again. His helplessness was showing beyond the bruises.

"I wish, but my mother won't let me fight. Not since I lost my father in the Siege of Palasera. She wants me to be a farmer instead. Live a life of silence and peace."

"Hey, I lost my father too. But I know it is my duty to keep his honor and uphold his legacy. My master always told me that the only way to make peace is to silence those inner demons."

The boy watched Moses closely and widened his eyes.

"Wait, aren't you the Chieftain's son?"

Moses nodded.

"Wow, I thought I would never meet someone like you up close. You're not even as pompous as I would've thought. Um… sorry about what I just said. I'm Korah by the way."

He extended his hand.

"Moses. It's good to meet you. And at such a good time as this."

Korah smiled shaking his hand.

"You know Moses, I think we could be best of friends."

***

Moses' thoughts lingered back to the present as he trailed behind his mother and brother. The silence was familiar, another voiceless journey. But it didn't trouble Moses. He no longer thought of the dream. His memory of meeting Korah on that day reminded him of how special he was despite Ramses' birthright as heir. Moses was special in his own way.

Chapter Nine

A Surprising Announcement

An hour has passed since Moses came back to the house. He was restless laying down on his bed with multiple thoughts in his head. He knew this day was going to be harsh. Especially now that he was caught, and no one wanted to hear him out. Ngozi was going to punish him. Give him more discipline and no telling what hardship was waiting for him. Sleep was out of the question.

"Moses, it's time to get up," said his mother. "I have breakfast ready for you and your brother. Make sure you eat. You need all your strength. Especially for today."

She walked away.

Moses let out a sigh then rolled out of the bed while rubbing his eyes. He reached to the top of the dresser across from his bed and grabbed his favorite blue cotton-wrapped pants that he uses for training. Moses opened a drawer beside him and grabbed a sleeveless combat training shirt made of kente cloth and placed it in a black backpack along with the pants.

He felt as if he was ready to drop. But Moses knew if he would pass out, he would later regret it. Moses quickly slipped on a lime green shirt with blue shorts and raced across the hall to the bathroom. He felt a hand beating his back. Ramses walked ahead of him and opened the bathroom door.

"Need to use the bathroom brother?" he grinned slamming the door in his face.

"Bastard," Moses muttered.

He entered the kitchen down from the small hall-way and sat on a wooden round table. Surrounding him were three plates of bread and eggs. No pastries. It's been seven days since his mother allowed him to eat sweets in the house. It felt like a punishment. Per-haps it was. Moses groaned and placed his head on the table. Then he felt a hard slap on the back of his neck that left a matching sting on his back.

"What did I tell you about placing your head on the table?" his mother said.

"But Mother, Ramses is taking a long time in the bathroom."

"What does that have to do with your attitude this morning?"

"I could've been washed up."

"Perhaps you should've done that when you decided to take a walk earlier this morning."

Moses let out a sigh, but his mother glared like a vicious predator. There was a time when Moses was his Mother's favorite child during the time his father was living. But in recent years Ramses became the favorite child since Moses began hanging out with Korah. She felt that Ramses was more focused and was the example of what a warrior and leader should be. Moses cuffed his hands on his head. At this point, he was ready to leave the house again.

Ramses sprang up on the kitchen table full of energy and life.

"Did anyone mention me?" he said staring at one of the plates.

"Ramses, we were actually waiting for you," said their mother.

Ramses placed his hand on his younger brother's back.

"Don't worry little brother," he said. "The trials are hard, but you will endure to the end."

Easy for you to say majesty, Moses thought wishing he could release the words.

Their mother joined them at the table.

"Now let us say our grace," she said. "Although Nubariah is lost, we must be thankful every day that we still have breath. Breath is hope, life. It is something the Spirit Mother Ala has granted us through the Spirit Father. Ramses, do the honor for us please."

Here we go again, Moses said in his head. *Let Ramses "the Great" say the blessing.*

Ramses and his mother bowed their heads. Moses was slumped on the table.

"Moses!" called his mother. "Either straighten up or you will get a beaten!"

Moses sighed and straightened up his body. He bowed his head listening in to the grace being spoken by his brother.

"Father Spirit Abiama, our Supreme God, thank you for another day of life. Bless us as we partake this food and bless our families. So be it."

Moses and his mother repeated. Everyone grabbed their forks and sunk their teeth into their meal except Moses. His mother scowled him in warning. Without a sound, Moses picked up the fork in front of him. It was an awkward silence as he bit small bites not budging to peek at his mother, especially his brother. Ramses took bite after bite devouring his plate. The clanking sound of the fork and plate left an eerie ring in Moses' ears. The smacking was far worse. His ears felt like they were about to explode.

His mother cleared her throat, breaking the silence that lingered at the breakfast table. Moses was feeling relieved.

"Ramses, what did I tell you about smacking at the table?" she said.

"My apologies Mother."

She wiped her mouth.

"And next time if you don't have to wash or use it, make sure you share the bathroom with your brother. You both are going to the same place."

"Yes, mother. I will next time."

A knock banged the front door. Their mother got up and walked out of the kitchen to see who decided to visit them abruptly in the early parts of the morning. Moses and Ramses were left by their selves.

There was silence again. Moses nibbled on a piece of bread refusing to look at his brother. Ramses took his final bites and dumped his plate in the sink. He grabbed his backpack and walked towards the back door.

"Tell Mother I'm out," he said.

Moses did not reply.

They heard multiple footsteps coming in their direction. Were they expecting company? Their mother walked into the kitchen with a gleaming smile accompanied by Ngozi.

"Master Ngozi," said Ramses bowing to him.

Moses got out of his seat and bowed in place.

"No need for that boys," he said. "I just came here with a big announcement before I head to the academy. I already told your mother."

"Yes, what is it Master Ngozi?" asked Ramses.

"The Council has spoken in an emergency meeting last evening. The Grand Guardian is soon ready to consecrate the heir of the throne."

Moses dropped his fork. The Grand Guardian? Heir? So soon? Those were questions filled in Moses' mind. It was rare for the Grand Guardian to appear unless there was a ceremony or coronation. Since the Shadow League's sacking of Palasera, the Grand

Guardian remained in Sahawayda along with the guardians. At a time, such as this, the Grand Guardian wants to make a visit and announce the heir? Moses knew it was his brother. The birthright was given to Ramses by his father as the firstborn son. His brother was ready. Ramses was mighty and a great leader that the entire village beloved. It made perfect sense that Ramses was chosen. He might be arrogant, but he always made sure to protect Moses and his mother.

Ramses grinned.

"So the time has come I see," he said. "And this soon? I guess my reputation has grown exponentially enough for the Grand Guardian to show his face. It looks like it's time to turn things up, right little bro?"

Ramses looked at his little brother and smirked. Moses smacked his lips, wishing his brother would go away.

"Do not let your arrogance outweigh your judgment," said Ngozi. "There's nothing worse in rulership than an arrogant king. An arrogant ruler always gets blind-sited by the enemy because he does not anticipate. In an arrogant man's eyes, he already has the victory of a battle that's uncertain. Remember this lesson, my pupil."

"Yes Master," said Ramses bowing.

Ramses kissed his mother on the cheek.

"See you later Mother and wish me luck," he said.

"I'll see you later Ramses," she said. "And be sure to watch over your brother during your training."

"I will Mother. I promise."

Ramses sauntered from the kitchen to the back door leaving Moses alone with his mother and Ngozi. Moses looked up, expecting his mother to scowl at him. But her face was straight, calm in a sense. There was silence again. Moses nibbled his food taking small bites.

"My apologies for not fixing you a plate Ngozi," said Moses' mother. "I wasn't expecting your company."

"It's okay Ashanti. I was making my way out. I have to make preparations in the School of Combat and Wisdom."

She sat back down on the table to finish her plate.

"Please, I insist," she said. "I'm sure you can get a little bit of rest before the day starts. Besides, I'm glad you're here. I have something to tell you about one of your pupils that is sitting at the table in front of you."

Ngozi turned his head to Moses.

Dang it, I thought she would have forgot, thought Moses.

"I guess I can stay for a few minutes," said Ngozi walking towards the table.

He pulled up a chair beside Moses. Ashanti took a couple of bites of eggs before letting out her concerns.

"Moses decided to go for another walk this morning," she said. "And he got himself into trouble again with that boy."

"So I see," said Ngozi.

He stared at Moses. Although he was looking down, Moses knew the intimidating look all too well. Moses' pulse was beating. He knew he was in trouble at this point. He stared at his plate. His appetite has completely vanished.

"What kind of trouble was he in this morning?" Ngozi questioned in a surprisingly calm state.

"Him and that boy went to some girl's house talking about marriage," said Ashanti.

"Wait what?"

Ngozi nearly choked on his words turning his head back to Moses. His looks were of shock and disappointment. Moses could sense it.

"Sounds like some foolishness Korah put Moses up to. He can't consider finding a wife until he is at least fourteen."

Ngozi studied Moses sounding a hum.

"I sense something else within him that's troubling," said Ngozi. "I've sensed it for a while. Do you mind leaving us alone for a moment Ashanti?"

"Of course," she said. "I respect your wisdom, Master Ngozi. I will leave you two alone while I tend to the flowers in the yard."

She got up from her seat and walked out of the kitchen leaving Ngozi alone with Moses.

Moses set his head straight. He sensed a calmness in Ngozi feeling nearly relieved that he did not announce a punishment. But he wasn't going to talk so soon. Ngozi was always hard on Moses pushing him almost past his limits physically, mentally, and spiritually. His punishments were merely brutal having to spend more hours in combat training and reading scrolls of the wise. Moses was expecting those tasks to be Ngozi's last words before ending whatever conversation he was stirring up.

"You are troubled boy," he said. "I sense a great disturbance within you. That is why you have not been focused these past few weeks. What is it that woes you so?"

Moses peered into Ngozi's eyes for a moment then he cuffed his hands back on his head letting out a deep breath.

"I know you say to let go of my feelings and sorrows, but at this point it is hard. I keep having these dreams about my fatha."

"Night terrors?"

Ngozi continued to study Moses as if he were reading his soul. Moses knew he couldn't hold his emotions in, not against Ngozi. He nodded his head in response. Ngozi rubbed his fingers on his goatee. He hummed.

"Tell me what happened in these recurring dreams," said Ngozi. "What did you all see?"

"I saw clouds of smoke around me. Then my fatha appeared. I was four years old again. Then I saw the throne. My fatha embraced me. Then a beast showed up. His terror was like the Shadow Lord. It choked the life out of my fatha. Then he promised to end me next. It's like it keeps happening over and over."

"What were your emotions?"

"It was fear, sadness, hope, relief, and horror."

Ngozi let out another hum.

"That means your destiny is coming to a head. You are dealing with the past of what was, the present of what is, and the future of what is to come. You will soon go through a great trial Moses. That is why in this time of season you must focus. Do not let your emotions get the best of you. Instead, harness and channel them. Use it as a weapon and not as a way of chaos. There is much danger and darkness within those thoughts that can cause you to implode or become a danger to others. Remember this wisdom I am giving you."

"Yes Master," said Moses.

No punishment? Moses nearly cracked a smile. He was on the clear.

"And by the way, after training this evening you are going to my house and study the scrolls based on the laws of marriage."

Moses sighed. He thought too soon.

His mother entered the kitchen from the back door.

"Moses, you need to hurry before you run late," she said. "And eat the rest of your food. You need your strength."

"Yes Mother," said Moses in a faint.

"It's okay, I'll give him a pass," said Ngozi. "He will come with me."

"Thank you for your kindness Ngozi," said Ashanti.

Moses took only a few more bites leaving half of the food on his plate. Moses got up from his seat and stretched. His mother was washing dishes.

"If you will not eat then go your way," she said. "I'm sure Ngozi would like to finish your food for you."

"I'm fine but thank you," said Ngozi.

Moses walked out of the kitchen to the hallway. He heard his mother calling from behind.

"Hurry boy! Ngozi is waiting for you!"

Moses rolled his eyes. He knew it was safe to do so since his back was turned from her. Moses entered the bathroom door, shutting it behind him.

After a few minutes of brushing his teeth and picking his hair, Moses emerged from the bathroom and slid on a pair of brown sandals. He grabbed the black backpack and headed back into the kitchen. Moses saw Ngozi and Ashanti sitting at the table grinning with cups in hand. They both spotted Moses walking in.

"Thank you again for the tea Ashanti," said Ngozi. "I see you are ready to go Moses. Let us depart."

"Yes master," said Moses.

"Remember to focus Moses," said Ashanti. "Both in your education and martial arts."

"Yes Mother, I will."

Ashanti embraced Moses and kissed him on the forehead.

"My baby," she said flashing her teeth.

Moses felt this day being strange already. His mother didn't call him her baby in a long time. First was the dream. Then the awkward moment earlier that morning when Korah tried to set him up with the rites of passage to marry the girl he did not like. And now the Grand Guardian's announcement. Moses wondered if his day was going to get any weirder. He was soon to find out as he followed Ngozi out of the door to get to the academy.

Chapter Ten

Heart Struck

While Moses accompanied Ngozi down the road, Ramses was on his way to the academy. The early morning crowd was lingering through the village. Kiosks of food, pastries, clothing, and jewelry were beginning to be crowded around each corner he turned. The elderly of the village and businessmen told him good morning. He could feel the respect of the people he was soon to rule over. He replied to the good mornings with confidence that he would become Nubariah's next great High Chieftain to overthrow Shadow Lord Mercius from the throne. A few young women around his age giggled at him with empty buckets in their hands.

"Hey Ramses," called out one of them.

"Morning ladies," he said.

Ramses knew of their flirtatious smiles and grins, but he had no interest in them. He wanted to find a woman that was worthy of him being his first lady.

Two young men dressed in dashikis approached Ramses and gave him daps.

"Ramses, what's good my man?" said one of the young men.

"All is good," said Ramses. "I hope you boys are ready for training today."

"Of course. Especially we got you on our corner."

"Ah don't put me on the pedestal fellas. When one of us dominates, we all dominate."

"Isn't that the truth."

"How about that little brother of yours?" asked the other young man.

Ramses was silent for a few seconds. His grin transitioned to a straight face of blankness from the thoughts of his brother.

"Moses can do what he wants," he said. "He has that waste of a friend Korah. Besides, I heard the Grand Guardian is coming today."

The young men paused. Their jaws dropped. Ramses broke their silence after a few moments.

"That's right. Master Ngozi told me and my brother that the Grand Guardian was coming to consecrate my father's heir."

"Well it's obvious that it's you," said the first young man. "I mean, your brother has the potential of becoming a great warrior, but he is far from being stronger than you. Besides, you have more favor over the people to rule. And not to forget you are the firstborn by right."

"Hey, your highness," said the other young man. "When you become new Chieftain, can I be your advisor?"

"Naw, I think he needs me as his advisor."

Ramses' grin returned. He wrapped his arms around both the young men's shoulders.

"I think both of you will make great advisors. As a ruler, I won't make you guys battle that position out. We're in this together."

Ramses gazed his eyes on a lone young woman ahead of him with two buckets in her hands. Her head was wrapped in a red covering. The dress she wore matched the covering with white, black, and orange textures. Her skin was like mocha. The young woman reminded him of Aminnaya. She was slightly older than him. He remembered her age, seventeen years old. Dayo was her name. He had to have her, especially now that he was about to become Nubariah's new Chieftain.

"Guys, I'll catch up to you at the academy," Ramses said. "I have a little business I must handle first."

The young men stared at Dayo and smiled.

"Go get her," they said.

Ramses departed from the young men and approached Dayo as she continued to walk about the village. He sped up, closing in to get her attention.

"Excuse me miss," he said. "Do you need assistance with those buckets?"

Dayo turned around startled but smiled when she saw Ramses.

"Ramses hello," she said. "It's good to see you."

"You as well Dayo. Do you need assistance?"

She shook her head.

"I'm fine but thank you. Shouldn't you be at the academy? I believe you're running late."

"I am on my way now. How about you? As intelligent as you are, I would have thought after the School of Basic Knowledge you would progress to the School of Advanced Knowledge and be a healer in the village."

"Well, I decided that medicine wasn't my strong suit. Besides, being a maiden is what I prefer anyways. I love taking care of the village this way. Me and the ladies are heading to the river to regenerate the panels right now. Oh, and where is your brother? I haven't seen him in a while."

"He's somewhere around here."

The small talk was beginning to agitate Ramses. He was in love with Dayo since he first laid his eyes on her for years now. He never had the confidence to tell her how much he felt about her despite his popularity and prestige. She was the daughter of Master Amazu the Lion Clan's new General and teacher in the School of Combat. He didn't want to blow the chance of being with her. He was a Lion, a warrior. He had to be courageous. He had to come into the mindset of Chieftain Ramses, and the Chieftain needed his rightful bride.

"Dayo there is something I must tell you," he said.

"Yes, what is wrong?" she asked.

"It's... I... Ever since I first met you, I couldn't help but to be amazed at your beauty."

Dayo blushed.

"Thank you, Ramses."

"No, that is not all. I... I was wondering if maybe, no..."

"Ramses just say it. There should be no shame."

"I want to be with you Dayo. I like you a lot."

Ramses couldn't believe he spewed the words. Those were words he was hoping not to regret. Dayo smiled. Perhaps there was hope.

"Ramses, that was sweet of what you said. But I'm married now."

Ramses froze. It was as if he was struck in the stomach by a bow.

"Oh, I didn't know. Well, congratulations. I thought you were supposed to get married after negotiating with the family. Did your father approve of your husband?"

"Thank you for your best wishes of me," she said. "Me and Tobukwu were able to get married. I mean, my father didn't approve of us getting married. He says my husband is weak, but he knows how to make me feel special you know."

She placed her hand on his shoulder.

"But don't give up Ramses. You're a big, beautiful, and handsome young man. There will be other young women that will want you. But I have to go okay. Best of luck in your training."

Dayo took the buckets and continued to carry them down the road. Ramses watched her walk away. His heart was broken. But he refused to feel defeated.

"You may be married, but I will not give up my love for you. You will be mine Dayo."

Chapter Eleven

Pressure

Moses followed Ngozi down the road carrying his backpack. It was moderately heavy. His books were blended with his training clothes. Moses was used to the walk. He walked to and from the academy three days a week in both the School of Knowledge and School of Combat. His thoughts outweighed the books he was carrying. His thoughts were blended between the Grand Guardian and the wisdom Ngozi gave him. Perhaps in a way, he was chosen. He might have to help his brother take down the Shadow Lord to save Nubariah. His role was just as important.

Moses looked up at Ngozi as people were greeting the martial arts master. For the first time, Moses felt important, although the attention was on Ngozi. Being in his very presence made him feel special.

"Master Ngozi," said Moses. "When is the Grand Guardian coming?"

"He hasn't said. The Grand Guardian is the eldest out of everyone in Nubariah. He is the overseer of Nubariah, chosen by the

Supreme. He never let anyone know when he comes. That is why when he makes the announcement, always prepare."

"Yes, master."

Moses was silent for a moment pondering in thought while his feet trailed behind Ngozi.

"How old is the Grand Guardian?" he wondered.

"Nobody actually knows," said Ngozi. "There are rumors that he lived for many centuries. He has acquired a lot of knowledge. He is the wisest man in Shiveria. Far wiser than I am."

"He sounds very intimidating," said Moses.

"He quite is. His power is limitless, but he's no warrior. Yet even a warrior knows not to cross him."

"Wow."

Moses would've thought he would be intimidated by the Grand Guardian, but he felt more excited. He figured he shouldn't feel this way, or perhaps he should. Regardless, Moses was thrilled. He could feel a change was coming. Rather the change would be for a better tomorrow or a graver future, this change was going to be better than his stagnant life in Dolsa. Moses continued to follow Ngozi down the road. They were only a few blocks away from the academy.

***

Ramses returned to his friends with a heaviness. He felt a defeat like never before. But he made a vow that he wouldn't give up no matter who she was married to, or who she may love for now. His love for her stemmed deeper than her temporary affection for another man.

"So, how did everything go?" said one of his friends.

"Find out she is married," said Ramses.

"Oh damn," said his other friend. "That has to be a blow for you. I'm so sorry. There will be another one."

"Yeah, you don't need her."

Ramses felt a desire further than any he felt. It was a burning passion like fire within brimstone. It was to the point where no one's words mattered but his undeniable love for what he now knows is a married woman. He had to have her. At this point, it was no matter the cost.

"But I will have her," he said. "No matter the cost."

"C'mon, you're about to be chieftain," said his friend. "You can have any woman you want. Why covet the wife of a low life?"

Ramses' lips wrinkled to a sly smirk.

"One thing to know about a king is that what he requests, he will get what he desires one way or the other."

His friends gave each other looks of unease.

"But enough of my love affair, let's get this day started shall we," said Ramses.

"Yeah, enough of these women. They are a distraction."

Ramses led the boys down the road striding with confidence despite the ache he felt internally.

***

Moses was a few miles away past the village of Dolsa's open field. Ahead of them were strips of grass with neem trees lined in rows. Beyond them stood the Dolsa Academy of Basic Learning. The academy was a multiplex of tan buildings designed with emerald roofs. The main entrance leads to the sports complex, dome, and lunchroom. The School of Combat was behind the main buildings that led to both the School of Knowledge and the School of Wisdom.

Moses continuously followed Ngozi to the academy watching young students talk amongst each other in their own groups. Some students walked past greeting Ngozi, but Moses was ignored. He was not popular in the academy, only being outshined by his older brother. His only supporter and friend that had his back was Korah. If only he wasn't much of a troublemaker. Moses was still upset about the incident from earlier that morning. It was an incident he was hoping to soon put behind and focus more on the bigger picture.

Moses walked side by side with Ngozi as they passed two more neem trees leading to a circle of concrete. They were at the main entrance of a roof connected to three buildings that blocked sunlight. It reminded Moses every day of the tunnel he and his family went through to escape from the Shadow Lord. Ngozi turned to Moses and placed his hand on his shoulder. Moses locked eyes with him.

"Remember Moses," he said. "Do not be discouraged of what you see before you. It is only for the moment. Instead, focus on what lies ahead."

"Yes master," said Moses.

Ngozi smiled and placed his fist on his chest. Moses did the same and walked his separate ways from Ngozi. The special moment drifted to a place of loneliness. How come it has to be this way? Being ignored, bullied by Ramses and his circle. Moses felt hated. He wanted to go home already. Then he heard someone calling his name amongst the crowd. Moses turned around and saw Korah waving at him. He nearly sighed and rolled his eyes, but instead, he sought out answers.

"Where were you?" questioned Moses. "I thought you would've bailed me out this morning."

"So, the guard caught you huh?" said Korah.

"Yes, he did. Then my mother and maddening brother showed up. So now I have to spend extra hours reading the scrolls of marriage."

"Well, at least you don't have to spend extra hours of discipline in the School of Combat. Master Amazu is showing no mercy."

"So, I guess you were caught too."

"Yeah. Onyeka's father wouldn't let up. He chased me down the road himself. To find out he was a guard off duty."

"Ouch. Sorry about that."

"Yeah, but that's behind us now."

Moses and Korah walked side by side heading towards the School of Knowledge. It was another day in the academy. Moses could feel the sunlight touching his face as he and Korah were at the end of the shaded entrance past the lunchroom. In front of them was a fleet of steps leading to a passageway of the three schools. The School of Knowledge was a long two-story dual building that had the capacity of 1,500 students split into two class levels. Moses was among the low-class level that was higher in education than the absolute beginners. He continued to compare himself to Ramses, the high-class level who only had a few years until he would graduate to the School of Advanced Knowledge and become a full-fledged warrior whether he was consecrated or not as chieftain. Moses cringed at the thought that his brother was always ahead of him in everything.

At the steps, Moses spotted Onyeka talking amongst a group of girls. He wanted to turn the other way. He did not want to be humiliated in front of his peers.

"Look it's Onyeka," said Korah.

"No, we should head to class," said Moses.

"C'mon, class is not in another ten minutes. You should talk to her."

"Not now Korah. Let's just c'mon."

Moses' eyes suddenly locked on Onyeka. He expected her to give him a stink look like usual, but today was different. She gazed at him in a mysterious expression that Moses thought was foreign. Moses didn't know what to do except place his head down.

"Just look at her she's digging you," said Korah.

"Or she's thinking about this morning."

Moses felt a hand from behind mushing the back of his head. Behind him was a group of laughter. He turned and saw Ramses and his friends smirking. Just when his morning couldn't get any worse, now he had to deal with his brother for the second time.

"So, what's going on little brother," said Ramses. "You're still hanging with this piece of trash."

"Oh Ramses," said Korah. "I think you was talking about your shit breath."

Moses giggled at the joke. Ramses glowered then curled his lips into a sneer.

"I have to admit that was a good comeback," he said. "It's too bad you can't do the same with your fighting skills. I see the words 'ass kicked' stamped on your forehead little farmer boy."

Ramses and his friends laughed with 'oooh' and dap hugs. Moses frowned keeping his guard up wishing he could punch his face. But now wasn't the time. Not during the hours of learning. He stepped up facing his brother despite his height and size. Ramses chuckled.

"You look like you want to do something brother," he said. "Make a move then. It's just like back in the palace when I made you cry like the punk you are."

Moses' blood boiled feeling the urge to hit him despite the academy rules. Students around them stopped watching the tension between the two with fascination. Moses saw on the corner of his eyes of Onyeka looking disgusted. This was not the attention he wanted this morning.

"Why won't you leave me alone Ramses," said Moses. "I don't feel like being bothered."

"Well, you don't have to be hostile towards me all the time. I can never have a basic conversation with you without you getting upset."

"Now you care about my feelings 'Mr. high and mighty'? Why won't you entertain your friends?"

Ramses grinned shaking his head.

"You just don't get it, do you. You never will. You are supposed to be of royal blood, but you sure as hell don't act like it."

Moses felt a fuse blow to the point he could care less about the academy rules. A nerve struck by his brother's words. He heard the students that gathered around them snigger. Moses cliched his jaw while pumping his fist. He pushed Ramses with all his force, and he stumbled back falling on the concrete. Ramses stared at Moses in shock. He didn't know whether to be angry or proud that his little brother had some courage. Ramses was somewhat embarrassed that Moses pushed him the way he did. He heard his friends in the background, "You're going to let him push you like that?" Ramses instead smiled while two administrators stood between the two. The monitor on Moses' side held him back from further contact.

"That's enough you two!" yelled the one of administrators standing in front of Ramses. "You two are brothers! So, act like it! And the rest of you clear out and head to class!"

The crowd dispersed. Moses turned and saw Onyeka shaking her head in disgust walking away. He felt shameful. The other administrator had let Moses go and turned his focus on him and his brother. Their friends were behind them.

"Just because you two are the sons of Oba, doesn't mean you have a free pass to disrupt the learning facilities," said the administrator. "Save your fighting later during the hours of combat. Do I make myself understood?"

Moses and Ramses, along with their friends, complied.

"I'm letting you off with a warning. Now get to class."

Moses watched as the school administrators walked away. He scowled at Ramses. They locked eyes for a final time before going their separate ways.

"This isn't over Moses," said Ramses. "Watch your back."

Moses watched his brother and his friends walk away towards the School of Knowledge. The crowd dispersed in an instant.

"I'm glad you stood up to that bastard," said Korah. "If he is to be our king and hope of saving Nubariah then we are in trouble."

A bell sounded that rang around the multiplex. A large hologram appeared over the rooftops of a man in a colorful suit of drapes. Moses recognized him as Administrator Chino, the dean's personal assistant. He knew it was time to head to class. He looked at Korah and nodded. They rushed towards the School of Knowledge overhearing what Administrator Chino was speaking through the hologram.

"Attention all faculty and students. I need you all to report to the dome for a special visitor. We are expecting everyone's attendance."

Administrator Chino disappeared from the hologram. Moses' felt his chest-beating in a rhythm. This had to be it. He felt a presence he never felt before. The thoughts crept thinking about Ngozi's words of wisdom concerning his recurring dreams.

"Well, at least we have a free bail from class," said Korah.

"Yeah, I know," was all Moses could say.

Moses could feel a cadence throbbing his chest as he and Korah walked towards the dome awaiting what lies within. It had to be his destiny, the fate that will change his life forever.

The Prophesy Unfolds

The crowd of students and faculty began to rush to the dome as Moses entered the tall, squared building alongside Korah. This was the third time Moses entered the dome. He was always mesmerized by the red carpet tracing the concrete floor and the ceiling made of bamboo with dim lights. It reminded him of home back in the palace although it was a long time ago since he breathed the fresh air of Palasera's ecofriendly atmosphere.

Moses spotted a double door beside him and entered in before the crowd gained in numbers. The arena was before him within the dome where musicals and rallies usually took place. Rows of seats were connected to form a square around the center stage where the administrators, the Dean, and the Council of Elders were sitting. Ngozi sat next to the Dean lost in his thoughts. He must have felt the same presence Moses felt.

"I think this spot is good," said Korah pointing to two seats in the fourth row. "I don't want to be some dork sitting in the front row."

"I agree with you on that," said Moses.

Moses led Korah to two seats in the fourth row that had a good view of the center stage. The crowd behind them increased taking seats row to row. Moses peaked and saw Onyeka walk with her friends down the steps to find a seat. She rolled her eyes at him with a smile. *What is her deal*? thought Moses while stooping his head. Ahead of him, he saw Ramses and his friends. He was thankful Ramses was seated on the other side of the arena.

"I bet this presentation's going to be dull," said Korah.

Moses thought differently. He didn't tell Korah yet that the Grand Guardian was possibly present. The words wanted to escape his breath, but he was too deep in thought. What if this was a coincidence and his mind was playing tricks on him? The Grand Guardian might not be here. But then Moses felt a powerful presence growing. It was intense. He quivered trying to hold himself.

"Are you okay Moses?" asked Korah.

Moses couldn't lie to his friend. Moses was close to Korah more than he would ever be with Ramses. He had to tell the truth.

"The Grand Guardian might be here."

Korah froze in a deep gasp.

"The Grand Guardian, here?"

"Master Ngozi told me and my brother he's coming."

"Then this changes everything."

The crowd was settling in as a few students slid past Moses and Korah to find a seat. A woman with long hair in a green textured dress of yellow and orange stood center stage in greeting then introducing the Dean. Moses was puzzled. The aura of this power was great within the arena, but no one on the stage carried it. Not even members of the Council. Something was off.

"And now I will give the stage to Dean Jelani," the woman said as the Dean got out of his seat and shook her hand.

He stood before the crowd.

"Brothers and sisters. Students and faculty alike," he said.

Moses continued to scan the arena. Rather it was the Grand Guardian or some other figure, he or she had to be somewhere amid the crowd. Moses' hearing of the Dean's speech was in and out.

"For seven long years, our people have gone through great oppression by the Shadow Lord's ruthless regime. But we are thankful for Lady Ashanti and Master Ngozi's efforts of making Dolsa a haven for refugees that escaped from servitude and captivity."

The Dean turned to Ngozi and nodded.

Moses continued to scan through the crowd. The presence of the powerful person was nowhere to be found. He turned around scanning through the crowd behind him. Then he felt Korah tapping him on his shoulder.

"Moses are you good?" he wondered. "You seem uneasy."

"I'm okay. I thought I saw something."

"It's the Grand Guardian isn't it?"

Then the Dean said something that caught Moses' attention.

"But now today we will push further. Because today we have a special visitor that will give us the wisdom and knowledge we need to take our nation back. So without further ado..."

This had to be it. Destiny was flashing before Moses' eyes, the destiny of what was, what is, and what is yet to come. His destiny was brought forth before his very eyes. This was the moment that would change Moses. He knew it someway and somehow. Moses leaned forward in the seat hearing the finishing of the Dean's warming speech.

"I would like to introduce to you all Grand Guardian Amine!"

Moses turned his head towards one of the tunnels. The power was drawing closer. The beats in his pulse increased.

Two men wearing white turbans and kaftans of gold linen appeared through the tunnel. Their beards were long and pointy. They had to be around the same age as Ngozi. The men were still in their young years, but they had a touch of gray on their beards. Moses could tell these were wise men, but they didn't wield the power he was sensing. Moses peered between the two men. There it was! Moses gasped. His body quivered. Walking between the men was the Grand Guardian himself. His presence was intimidating. His youth was past him, but time was like his best friend. His beard was white and wooly as a sheep. His skin was rugged, but he was nothing like the elderly Moses usually sees every day. He was different. Moses heard the united gasps around the arena. There was utter silence as everyone stood to their feet, including the Council to witness the majestic presence of his blue and white kaftan. The blue turban on his head was like a crown decked in gold. The white locks in his hair flashed from the back of the turban.

Moses could tell his wisdom and power far exceeded anyone Shiveria has ever imagined. And here he was, present in front of the public. Moses and everyone in the arena from the students to the administrators and council stood in awe as the Grand Guardian made his way to the center stage.

One of the men escorting the Grand Guardian waved his hand down as everyone took a seat. Moses followed suit, amazed by the Grand Guardian's presence. The Grand Guardian stood in front of the audience with looks of intensity. There was a pause as silence lingered in the atmosphere like a cloud of mist. Moses leaned to his seat. He felt beats in his chest. His body temperature was increasing feeling droplets of sweat around his body. His stomach was weak. His legs were trembling as if a chill went through him. Then the Grand Guardian spoke.

"Brothers and sisters," the Grand Guardian said. "Children of the Supreme God Abiama!"

He paused again. Moses could feel the fear around the arena through the silence of everyone anticipating what the Grand Guardian would say next. The Grand Guardian rubbed his white beard. Moses peered at Ngozi. He could tell he was trembling inside. The Grand Guardian finally spoke again.

"He has spoken."

Moses gasped within a multitude of gasps and whispers surrounding him. Everyone knew who "He" was. It was the Supreme God himself that gave the Grand Guardian a vision of what was soon to come. The atmosphere around the arena created a place of anxiety as the Grand Guardian continued.

"I know your suffrage. I know your oppression. I have felt your pain. And now the Heir of Oba is ready to rise to free Nubariah."

There were whispers again. Moses looked across the arena at his brother. Moses looked at his determined look. The consecration was beginning. Destiny was beginning.

"The man child from Oba's seed will defeat the Shadow Lord. He will be mighty, wise. His power will exceed the Shadow Lord's. The man-child's power will exceed that of his father's. This power... is universal."

The arena was full of awe and shock as Moses' chest thumped. He almost couldn't breathe. Universal power? That type of power was only wielded by the gods. No terrestrial in the history of any clan wielded such power except Chukwu, the progenitor that Moses knew very little about. Moses was intimidated. Was his brother deemed that powerful? The Grand Guardian now had the face of assurance.

"Ramses, take a stand!"

Ramses got up from his seat. He saw the crowd reveling him in wonderment. His friends patted him on the back in celebration.

"You got this Ramses," one of his friends said.

He heard the crowd cheering. Some people were chanting his name. Others were screaming, "My king!" or "My savior!" Ramses placed his fist up, the noise of the arena boomed like thunder.

"Moses!" yelled the Grand Guardian. "Will you stand!"

The arena fell silent. Ramses smile dropped to a glare. Moses shuddered as he stood to his feet. There were whispers again. Korah burst into a yell of support patting Moses on the back.

"Yeah, Moses!" he yelled. But there were only a few handclaps. Korah fell silent with the rest of the crowd.

The Grand Guardian stared at Moses and Ramses, then continued.

"You two are the seed of Oba. But only one of you is chosen. One will take back the throne. The other will be made into a Chief Prince. I am issuing a challenge for both of you. You will face each other in hand-to-hand combat of Kung Dambe. One brother will be stronger than the other, wiser than the other, more powerful than the other. The Supreme God will reveal it. You both have one day to prepare. I will speak no more."

The Grand Guardian walked off the stage accompanied by the two strange men. Administrator Chino rose from his seat to address the startled crowd as the whispers became echoes of loud conversation. Moses and Ramses remained standing eyeing each other.

"All students head to your class," said Chino. "Classes will resume as scheduled."

The crowd began to disperse. Moses glared at his brother's intensifying looks. The expression on his face was something that Moses had never seen before. It was as if he was out for blood. Tension beamed in the emptying arena. Destiny was becoming clearer. Moses knew now that he had to take the birthright from his brother to fulfill what was prophesied to him as the distant face-off continued.

Chapter Thirteen

The First Test

I can't believe the level of disrespect I just received out there!" hollered Ramses slamming his fist on a titanium locker next to him.

A few hours have passed since the Grand Guardian announced his prophecy to both the school, and the entire village of Dolsa through Optix projectors. Ramses and his friends were in an abandoned locker room of dim lights. Ramses was triggered. He never had let anything spark him at a rage so high. But this time he was greatly insulted. His moment was tainted. His momentum faded to darkness. His friends backed away. He saw their fear but cared less. The locker he slammed was dented by his undeniable strength.

"I am the chosen seed of the throne by right! What does that old man know! What type of God would deny the next king in line! My little brother dares to challenge me for the throne? That scrawny little pest who wastes his time with low-level trash like Korah! The boy can't even get a basic exercise right!"

"Ramses calm down you're better than this," pleaded one of his friends.

Ramses paced back and forth still enraged puffing short breaths. His friend tried touching him on the shoulder, but he jerked it away. His other friend stepped up to him with caution.

"The Grand Guardian did say one of you will be the heir. Show the people who really deserves the throne."

Ramses stopped. He stared at his friends and nodded in agreement.

"You're right," he said. "First I'm going to embarrass him. Then after I'm done beating him, I'll make him beg for mercy. And then I will make him bow down to his king."

Ramses and his friends smiled mischievously.

"Long live the Chieftain, King Ramses the Mighty," said his friend.

"King Ramses the Mighty," said Ramses. "I like that."

They sat together on a bench, continuing their plans for rulership until the next bell rang for class.

***

Moses sat on the desk twiddling his fingers. Usually, he enjoys Law and Government class. It was his favorite subject. But he couldn't get the image of his brother out of his head. He couldn't stop thinking of the anger, the hateful glare in his eyes. Ramses was always annoying, but this was another side that was introduced to Moses. He was out for blood and Moses was the target. He felt as if his pulse ceased from wanting to beat. He never felt such pressure. Even if he could overcome his brother, how could he rule a nation? Better yet, how could he have the power to defeat the Shadow Lord? His thoughts were like a whirlwind. He was overwhelmed. Moses rose his head in alarm feeling a tap on his shoulder. He turned around and saw Onyeka looking at him. *Why do she have to bother me now*, he thought.

"I hope you beat your brother tomorrow," she whispered. "A jerk like him doesn't deserve to be our king."

"Thank you," Moses replied.

"Moses Ezenwa," said Instructor Okorie. "Perhaps you would like to volunteer."

Moses immediately came out of his trance and focused his attention on the instructor. He had a pen in his hand to control the holoprojector in the class. Moses spotted a question referring to the original Laws of Ouidah before the Shadow League's conquest.

"What is the consequence of the law that dictates all those found guilty of theft from private property?"

Moses began to get agitated. As if this day couldn't get any worse, now teachers were beginning to pick at him. He wished that his life would go back to normal where he was invisible towards society.

"You're just calling me out because the Grand Guardian chose me as well to challenge for the throne," said Moses. "I guess teachers feel a kind of way with this too."

The class was sniggering at Moses' response. Instructor Okorie scowled.

"Excuse me?" he questioned. "So, do I have to report this to your master?"

Moses sighed. The least he needed right now was Ngozi punishing him for misbehaving in a class such as this. He peered at the holoprojector. He knew the answer, but he didn't feel like answering it. He just wanted to be left alone.

"I don't know," he said.

Instructor Okorie studied him.

"You don't know. I see," he said twisting the pen in his hand. "Perhaps you lost focus today. Can anyone tell Moses of the law that dictates all those found guilty of theft from private property?"

A student raised her hand with puffs in her hair sitting near the front row. The instructor pointed in her direction.

"The Law of Ouidah that dictates all those found guilty of theft from private property faces the consequence of 'eye for an eye'," she said.

"Very good," said Instructor Okorie. "If anyone in Palasera or anyone within Ouidah that would be found guilty of theft within a private property would face the judges and they would rule in the favor of the defendant an eye for an eye, meaning if you steal something valuable like a family heirloom, that person could take whatever that person has if they don't pay a reimbursement of the stolen item."

The bell rang abruptly ending class for the day. The students got up from their seats as the instructor got everyone's attention. Moses was ready to leave. He was waiting for this day to end.

"Don't forget you have a quiz Friday. And Moses, I expect better from you next time."

Moses clenched his jaw and swung his backpack on his back. He rushed out of the classroom vanishing within the crowded hall until he got to his locker. He felt someone tapping on his shoulder as he placed a few books in his locker.

"Not now Korah, I have things to do."

Moses turned around and paused staring at Onyeka in front of him.

"Onyeka?" he questioned. "What do you want with me?"

She smiled while rolling her eyes in a smile.

"Listen, before things get weird, I just want to say thank you about this morning. What you did back there was sweet, and it made me feel special."

Moses felt a warmth within himself that he never felt before. It was a tingling feeling that felt weird. He wanted to say words like "you're welcome" but this conversation was too good to be true. Onyeka to Moses was the girl who would pick on him for no reason and embarrass him with every opportunity she would get. He glared at her.

"Korah put you up to this didn't he?" he questioned.

Onyeka sighed, her smile disappearing.

"See, this is what I'm talking about right here. You're so up-tight. Just... never mind."

Onyeka walked away. Moses could tell she was serious, and she was right. He began to feel a soft spot inside him that was hardened for a long time. Moses chased after her and grabbed her arm.

"Wait Onyeka," he said.

She turned and faced him.

"I'm sorry for what I just said. I can tell that you mean what you say. Korah did set the whole thing up this morning because he felt that we would be perfect together. And I don't know. He could be right... or not. But I'm not ready for that kind of thing."

Onyeka smiled with certainty.

"Only time can tell. But if you would ask me for marriage I would say yes. Not because you're the son of the chieftain and could win against your brother, but I can tell that you're really sweet deep inside. You're different."

Moses felt a tingle in his cheeks. It was another weird feeling to have.

"Thank you Onyeka," he said. "I best better be going now."

"Me too. And if you ever mention this to anyone, even Korah, I will rip your lips off your face."

"Right."

Moses grinned and went his separate ways from Onyeka.

***

Hours have passed, but it felt like days for Moses. The day ended for the School of Knowledge, but the School of Combat was soon to begin with another lesson. Moses was not ready to endure what lied between those double doors. He was already dressed in his combat shirt and blue cotton pants. The academy was clearing out as the majority of students left to go back to the village leaving young warriors for training behind. Moses peeked at two young men dressed in long dashiki suits heading to the School of Wisdom where the young hopefuls trained to become priests. At this moment he wished he could run in their direction.

"Hey, young Oba!" called out one of the young men.

Moses turned his head in alert.

"Best of luck to you tomorrow against your brother."

"Thank you," said Moses although he didn't mean it.

In Nubariah, especially in Ouidah, luck was an insult. Moses could tell even the young priests had little faith in him. Perhaps his faith was dwindling. Moses was about to face one of the toughest challenges in his life. Even if he could manage to defeat his brother, the pressure would be greater on him because his nation would be counting on him to free them from the Shadow Lord. The very same Shadow Lord he must someday confront that killed his father before his very eyes. He stared at the double doors again and gulped.

C'mon Moses, you can do this, he thought.

Moses opened the door as the light in the lobby beamed in his face. He stepped in as a young woman appearing in her late teens sat at a desk catching his attention.

"You better hurry Moses, the masters are waiting for you. How things are looking, this training session is very serious. I wouldn't want to be late for this one."

"I'm here now," he said rushing past her.

Ngozi rushed through a steel door in urgency. He scowled at Moses the moment he spotted him.

"Boy where have you been?" he asked. "The Council is waiting for you."

"I'm here Master Ngozi," said Moses.

"Well c'mon."

Moses followed Ngozi as he rushed through the door. Moses entered a complex with a sunroof. The air he felt in the lobby was engulfed by the greenhouse effect of the outdoor facility. The Lion's Den is what they called the training grounds. The ground was covered in red dirt like the roads passing the village with small patches of grass. Moses saw all the pupils kneel in a circle around the Council members.

"Moses Ezenwa!" called Master Amazu within the circle. "Come!"

He wore a silk gold-like kufi hat with a sleeveless silk robe and a long white shirt underneath. The other Council members were dressed the same. He glared at Moses, but his glare was calmer than Ngozi's. He was far more patient. His salt and pepper beard seemed to be the confirmation that Amazu should be the head of the council instead of Ngozi, who only had a touch of grey. But Ngozi was close to the royal family and he had a better spiritual insight than any of the Council members. Ngozi joined the circle with the rest of the Council. Moses was cautious of who he was going to take a kneel beside. He scanned the circle to spot where his brother was located. He couldn't miss it. Ramses stared him down with the same intense look from back in the dome. Moses joined in the circle from the opposite direction of where Ramses was kneeling next to his friends.

Amazu opened his mouth again to speak. Moses focused, ignoring his brother's malice stare.

"Ngozi is supposed to address this with you all since he's the head of the Council," he said. "But he left that up to me and trust in my knowledge of the throne's history. Now today the Grand Guardian has spoken. The seed of Oba will arise after tomorrow. Usually, a chieftain rules for thirty up to fifty years until he retires and passes the throne to his heir. Unfortunately, we lost our chieftain prematurely due to the hands of our enemies. We were all in shock at the prophecy that was spoken to us today, but we can't underestimate the Grand Guardian's wisdom of what he has from our Supreme God. Ramses or Moses will become our new chieftain and challenge the Shadow Lord. Boys, stand and join us."

Moses exhaled breath as he got up and joined the Council. Ramses stood three feet from him, not looking at him at all. Moses felt his pulse thrashing. Ngozi stepped up to speak.

"Today's training will revolve around the two of you. First, your might will be tested. Then your mind."

Ngozi motioned two volunteers from the militia to step in front of the boys. They were young men older than Ramses by a few years. Moses recognized them as students that graduated from the School of Combat last year who recently joined Dolsa's militia. The young men took off their shirts revealing their cut muscles. Moses quivered. Was he to fight them before his brother?

"In order to defend a nation, a leader must learn to defend themselves," said Ngozi. "Ramses, Moses, you must hold your guard against these young warriors. Counter if you see an opening."

"Yes master," said Ramses in a dark but sharp tone.

Moses nodded, unable to speak a single word.

"Who would like to volunteer?" asked Ngozi.

"I will," said Ramses stepping up.

He took off his shirt brushing past Moses. The cuts in his muscles matched the young man's. He stretched his arms and legs while Moses and everyone in the gym backed away giving them space. Ramses bent his knees and pumped his fists. He neither flinched nor showed signs of fear. The only thing on his mind was vengeance.

"Ready," said Ngozi. "Commence!"

Moses watched as the young man moved forward holding his guard. Ramses held his guard unfazed by the young man's movements. He threw swift punches at Ramses that made sounds like a violent wind. Ramses remained focused dodging and blocking each punch from the body to the face. Ramses planted his foot and dodged out of the way from another punch. He stared at the young man's jaw and unleashed a powerful jab that slammed him to the floor. Everyone was silent, astonished at how Ramses was able to knock the advanced warrior out so quickly. Moses was discouraged. That could be him tomorrow. Ramses shrieked out a war cry flexing his muscles. His ponytail locs were still intact. Ngozi waved him off.

"Enough Ramses," he said. "You have passed the first test."

Ngozi gestured one of the pupils in the circle to seek medical aid for the young man. Two other pupils grabbed the young man and dragged him out of the circle. Ngozi looked in Moses' direction.

"Moses," he said. "Step up, you're next."

Moses was terrified staring at the young man. This was his first-time sparring, better yet fighting someone older than him besides the years he trained with his brother. The other young man was twice the size of him. Moses stared at his athletic body of muscular arms and eight packed abs. Moses was cut for his age, but his body didn't match with his opponent's. In his mind, he wanted to run. He wanted out from the challenge against his brother. But as a possible future leader, he had to show courage. The Council was watching him. The Grand Guardian was watching him. Moses slowly took off his shirt revealing his six-pack. He slowly stepped up to the young man and steadily got into his fighting stance.

"Don't hold back on this young one," said Ngozi referring to Moses.

Moses gulped. He thought of a time when Ngozi gave him encouraging words during training. He could hear the voice in his head.

Remember to focus Moses. Focus on your opponent. Channel his movements. It's all in the mind first.

Moses took a deep breath and locked eyes on his opponent.

"Ready," said Ngozi. "Commence!"

The young man stared down at Moses as if he was studying him. Perhaps he was. It was a temporary stare-down until the young man threw a low kick to Moses' left leg. Moses read the young man's movements and leaped out of the way. Everyone in the gym whispered amongst each other except Ramses who glared at Moses. The young man caught Moses off guard using swift movements of punches. Moses barely blocked them feeling a sharp pain in his arm from where the punches landed. He lost his balance and fell to the ground. The young man stared down Moses preparing for a strike. He thought of something fast on instinct, so the young man won't give the striking blow. He threw his legs up and kicked the young man in the stomach before he could strike. The young man held his stomach taking short breaths while wincing.

Ngozi waved his hand.

"That's enough," he said. "Moses, you have passed."

Everyone in the gym clapped except Ramses. The Council stepped in to join Ngozi. The young man helped Moses to his feet. He leaned to Moses' ear in a whisper.

"Focus as you did against me today," he said. "Your brother is a heavy striker, but you have the best defense. Use that against him."

Moses nodded as the young man walked away. He joined in the circle and focused on the Council as Ngozi spoke.

"Now that the first test is complete, the second test will begin. Moses, Ramses only one of you will pass the next test. I challenge you both to meditate on the words I am giving you. So listen to the words of the ancient ones: 'Only the humble, the strong, and pure of heart can exceed the rulership as high chieftain and Nubariah's king. Tomorrow's challenge is that second test, it all begins with the mind before the physical manifestation. May the Supreme watch over you both."

The Council dismissed the pupils as Moses turned his attention to Ngozi.

"You did well today, Moses," he said. "You have made everyone in here a believer. I'm proud of you."

"Thank you, master," said Moses. "Am I still to study the laws of marriage with you?"

Ngozi shook his head.

"Go home and rest up for tomorrow. You need your strength."

Moses nodded and grabbed his shirt, putting it back on. He grabbed his backpack and exited the gym.

"Wow Moses, you did great back there," said Korah as Moses made his way outside.

"Thank you Korah," he said.

"How you were able to hang with a warrior from the militia? I think you have a chance against your brother."

"I barely was able to defend myself back there. My fight with my brother will be a full fight. Anything goes. I will have to do more than defend myself."

"Hey, I believe in you, just believe in yourself."

Korah placed his hand on Moses' back. Moses smiled knowing he had someone to believe in him. The door to the School of Combat opened. Amazu came out with two pupils carrying wooden staffs.

"Korah, don't think I'm letting you off the hook," he said. "Your punishment begins now."

Korah turned his head to Moses with looks of disdain.

"You're so lucky you don't have to deal with punishment today," he said.

He took a few steps forward and turned around. Moses could feel his pain, but the pressure he felt outweighed a single punishment.

"But today it's on me. You did more for me than anyone would do for a lifetime. And as far as it goes this morning, thank you for having my back. You are a true friend. I hope you beat that bastard tomorrow."

Korah turned back to face his punishment from the trouble he stirred up earlier that morning. Moses let out another smile and left to go back to the village. He was alone once again.

Chapter Fourteen

Clash of Rulers

It had been a few hours since Moses came back home. The day was officially over with nightfall shining in the dark sky. There was great tension in the house. Moses could feel it as he laid in his bed after taking a warm shower. He hadn't seen his brother since earlier that day when he knocked the young warrior out in the School of Combat. He knew Ramses was home. He could hear the slams outside the hallway and murmurs between him and his mother. Moses didn't want to see him either. He was relieved to only see his mother sitting at the kitchen table when she asked him about his day when he walked through the kitchen door after school and training. Even during that time, his brother didn't show his face. This evening was different for Moses. Usually, his brother would come home to bear hug him or give him a nuggy which always made his hair nappier. For some odd reason, Moses preferred that over the high tension swarming the house.

Moses meditated in his head of a strategy to possibly slow down his brother. But he couldn't focus on the task. He was more fearful. This wasn't a friendly competition. He knew his brother was out for blood. He took a deep breath and closed his eyes. He could hear the words of Ngozi again ringing in his head like an alarm.

Remember to focus Moses. Focus on your opponent. Channel his movements. It's all in the mind first.

He thought of the warrior he sparred with earlier and how the young man overpowered him, but he couldn't get past his defense. Moses thought of that same move being a possible way to catch Ramses off guard.

"Moses," said the voice of his mother.

He turned his head and saw her at the doorway.

"Dinner is ready," she said sincerely.

Moses could tell the war between him and his brother was disturbing to her. He could tell by looking at the sorrow in her eyes as she walked past the kitchen.

Moses washed his hands undisturbed. Ramses was still nowhere to be found. At this point he had to be playing mind games, leaving Moses in a state of fear and panic before tomorrow's challenge. Moses took a deep breath. He wasn't going to get manipulated. After he dried his hands, Moses went into the kitchen, his plate was already at the table. It was his favorite, Abacha and Ugba. His mouth watered for the sundried cassava flakes blended in with oil bean seed and fresh vegetables. The plate was topped with fried fish which was his mother's specialty.

His mother was the only person sitting at the table. There was no third plate waiting for Ramses. Moses sat across the table from his mother as she said a silent prayer to herself. They were silent for a moment eating. Moses stared at a colorful scarf wrapped around his mother's braided hair. She smiled at him while chewing her food. For the first in a long time, she saw him as her baby instead of a young militant.

"As you can see Ramses will not be joining us for dinner," she said. "Your brother has been in and out of the house since coming back from training. He hasn't returned yet, but I'm going to leave him alone. I know a lot is on his mind since what transpired today."

Yeah, have pity on that spoiled brat, thought Moses in his head. *If that were me, I would get scolded.*

"I remember the day I gave birth to you. Your father expected a girl because Ramses was already his chosen heir. But the Supreme had other plans. Me and your father always knew something was special about you from the moment you were out my womb. Ngozi even sensed it. It only hit me today when the Grand Guardian announced you were chosen as well."

"So, do you think I will stand a chance against Ramses?" asked Moses.

Her smile transitioned to a frown as she took a bite of one of the fish on her plate before responding.

"You both are my sons and I love you all equally. You and Ramses have made your father proud. But I can't tell you what will happen tomorrow. The Supreme is in control of everything. He will decide the victor between you two and it will show. But despite what happens tomorrow, you two are still brothers and you should love each other no matter the outcome."

Moses nodded his head with approval while chewing on the sundried cassava sticks. They were silent again. Moses barely had an appetite despite his favorite meal being in front of him besides pastries.

"Eat as much as you can," said his mother. "You will need your strength."

After dinner, Moses went back to his room and laid on his back placing his hands behind his head. He stared at the full moonlighting in the night sky through his window. The stars were scattered around it like glitter glistening in a portrait of wonder to behold. Moses' mind was pondering as if it was dashing in the wind. He thought of the dream he had the previous night and how Ngozi linked it with a destiny he knew little about. He thought about the Grand Guardian and his name being announced as a challenge to Ramses for the birthright of the throne. He thought of the rage his brother had when he knocked unconscious the young warrior. That could be him tomorrow. Then the thought of Ngozi came into his mind like a soothing tune.

That means your destiny is coming to a head. You are dealing with the past of what was, the present of what is, and the future of what is to come. You will soon go through a great trial Moses. That is why in this time of season you must focus. Do not let your emotions get the best of you. Instead, harness and channel them. Use it as a weapon and not as a way of chaos. There is much danger and darkness within those thoughts that can cause you to implode or become a danger to others. Remember this wisdom I am giving you.

Moses let out a smile and closed his eyes, drifting off to sleep.

***

Night had turned back to the day as the morning drifted. Moses wished time would slow itself down, but destiny was not waiting for him. He once again followed his morning routine of picking out his clothes, brushing his teeth, and having breakfast time with his family. Today was like no other. Moses looked at his blue cotton pants and shook his head. If he was competing to be the new High Chieftain, he had to wear something more ceremonial to dress the part. He saw in his closet an all-white outfit with a blue silk belt and long white turban that he only wore once during the Ouidah holiday of the Celebration of Faith the past winter. This was what he needed. Moses had put on the outfit draping a brown beaded necklace around his neck. He went into the kitchen. No plates were sitting before him at the table. Perhaps his mother was just as nervous as him and forgot to cook. He did smell the scent of akara lingering in the kitchen which made his stomach turn. His mother appeared from the living room.

"I've received a message from Ngozi," she said. "The challenge will begin in a few hours."

"What?" questioned Moses. "I thought we would have the challenge during the hours of combat."

"The Grand Guardian wastes no time."

"Good, the sooner the better," said Ramses coming from the hallway.

Ramses wore a black and gold kaftan and black pants. His red beaded necklace matched with the red ozo hat he was wearing. He walked past Moses without acknowledging him.

"You wear that hat as if you are already chief," said their mother. "You should take it off until you are consecrated. You don't want any of the Council to catch you with it on, especially Ngozi."

"Nonsense Mother," said Ramses. "By right I am chieftain. I just have to make an example today. I do hope that you have breakfast ready for me Mother. I don't want to waste any time."

She sighed shaking her head. She spoke in Igbo muttering.

Nwa mpako. Arrogant child.

"Breakfast is already ready in the oven for you and Moses. I would fix your plates but you both will have to take them to go."

"Already ahead of you."

Ramses opened a drawer and pulled out a cloth. He grabbed six akara, placing them in a cloth. Ramses wrapped his arm around his mother and kissed her on the cheek.

"See you later Mother," he said. "Next time you see me, I'll be the deemed chieftain. I promise I will make you and Father proud. And when I do become chieftain, I promise that I will avenge Father and our people by killing the Shadow Lords, starting with Mercius."

She nodded her head with approval, but with a distant look.

"I'll see you later my sweet," she said.

Ramses smiled and walked out of the door. Moses glared at him. It was as if Ramses tossed him away like trash. What was worse was that the ozo hat he had on was made for only chieftains, something Ramses wasn't officially. Moses felt disrespected. At this point, he had to win. He too was the son of Oba, the next generation of the Ezenwa family.

"You should go too Moses. You don't want to be late."

"Will you come see the challenge Mother?" he asked.

She cracked a smile, but her eyes were sorrowful.

"I'll come; I promise."

Moses dashed and hugged her. She squeezed him, kissing him on his forehead.

"Now go. Make me and your father proud."

Moses smiled and grabbed a couple of akara from the oven and walked out of the door leaving his mother alone.

It was moments later that Moses made his way inside the complex. Korah was beside him as he sat on a bench in the locker room separate from his brother. He could hear the crowd growing, anticipating who will be their next chieftain. Moses knew the entire village was watching. Perhaps the word of the Grand Guardian traveled throughout Nubariah. He felt as if he was a prisoner waiting for a death sentence. Having the butterfly stomach effect was an understatement. Korah placed his hand on Moses' back.

"Don't worry Moses," he said. "You got this."

Moses nodded his head with assurance.

"Moses," said a man appearing from the entrance of the locker room.

He could recognize him as one of the men in all white accompanying the Grand Guardian. Moses' chest was thumping. It was as if his throat was catching fire thinking of the crowd that was awaiting him. The entire village must be present. Moses got up from the bench getting the man's attention.

"It is time," he said gesturing Moses to follow him.

The man turned his attention to Korah.

"Son, you will have to join the others in the gym. Only the royal seed can be present back here."

"Hey, Moses is my best friend and his only support that's on his corner," said Korah. "I won't let him face this alone."

The man smiled and nodded.

"So be it."

The man led Moses out of the locker room down the hall. Although Korah was with him, Moses couldn't help but feel an undeniable pressure. His destiny was out there. His world was about to change. This was happening so fast. There was no time to prepare for this moment. The man guided him to a double door in the lobby. A few other men dressed in white kaftans joined them. The noise of the crowd grew louder. He could hear the chants in Igbo, *Ekele dịrị onye isi ọhụụ* (Hail to the new chief). *Eze anyị ga-azọpụta anyị* (Our king will save us). The men nodded at each other. Moses took a deep breath ignoring his surroundings. The man opened the doors revealing the anticipated crowd surrounding them. Cheers abrupted like a raging storm. Moses could tell there was a blending in the crowd. He could see students, instructors, businesspeople from the kiosks, guards, and militia. Moses was led to a square platform with four red poles on each corner. He walked up four steps leading him inside the platform. From the opposite end of where Moses was standing, Ramses entered the platform barefoot in his black kaftan. His pony tail were loose revealing his long locs that touched his back.

Moses saw the men sitting next to the Grand Guardian. The Council was seated around the platform in a semi-circle spectating the challenge. Then there was the beating of drums as young women in colorful dashiki dresses emerged on the platform dancing to the rhythm. Moses meditated for a moment clearing out the noises of the crowd, the loud drums, the young women chanting in their dance. He focused his mind on Ramses. He sensed out his rage, his arrogance. That must be his weakness.

The drums stopped. The women bowed to Moses and Ramses then the Grand Guardian before departing off the platform. The crowd was silent as a man in a rose-colored suit with a blue shirt of rose linen stepped in to address the crowd. Moses stared at the ozo on his head that matched his suit.

"Ladies and gentlemen," the man said. "Boys and girls. This is the moment you've all been waiting for. Today marks the day of our new beginning, but who will be our true rightful Chieftain? Which child of the Ezenwa bloodline will take their rightful place? Will it be the chosen heir Ramses of Oba?"

Cheers abrupted in the crowd. Moses nearly rolled his eyes when he heard young ladies screaming.

"Or does our Supreme God choose the unexpected, the second-born son of Oba, Moses!"

There were fewer cheers than the previous. Korah shouted his name behind him. Moses could sense the crowd being less desirable of him winning the challenge. He took off his sandals and unwrapped his turban handing them to Korah. Across from him, Ramses took off his kaftan revealing his bare muscular features. Moses took off his shirt and brown beads while Korah wrapped his arms with a blue wrist bracer.

"You got this," said Korah.

Moses nodded his head and stepped up to face his older brother. He too had on a wrist bracer, but it was gold. They were face to face in the middle of the platform. The man in the rose-colored suit was gone, replaced by another man who was refereeing the challenge.

"The challenge has officially begun," he said to the boys. "Remember to fight with honor. The winner will emerge as the one who incapacitates his opponent."

The man backed away and left the boys staring into each other's eyes in both rage and focus.

"You have a chance now to back away," said Ramses. "Save yourself the embarrassment and accept me as your king."

"I must follow my own destiny," said Moses.

"Then you are a fool."

Ramses got into his fighting position. Moses did the same focusing on his brother's body movements. He breathed through his nose, erasing any type of emotion he had.

"Ready!" yelled the man. "Commence!"

Moses studied Ramses closely. Ramses pumped his fist aiming to land a powerful punch at his younger brother. Moses flinched planting his right foot anticipating a punch to his face or body. Instead, Ramses used his leg strength to kick the back of Moses' ankle as he fell hard on the mat. *Oooouuu!* were the shouts of the crowd. Ramses walked away shaking his head. Moses felt ringing in his ears with the blending of sounds as his head spun in blurs of flashes. He could hear Korah shouting, "Get up Moses!" He heard young women in the crowd saying, "Boy stay down." Then he heard his mother's voice in his head, *Me and your father always knew something was special about you from the moment you were out my womb. Ngozi even sensed it.* Moses grunted. His vision was clearing as the referee stood above him.

"Moses are you alright?" he said.

He nodded and sat up. Ramses glared at him as he slowly stood to his feet. *"Onye nzuzu,"* said Ramses in Igbo referring to Moses as a stupid fool.

Moses got back into his fighting position. Ramses smirked then he directly attacked Moses with a series of punches. Moses put his arms up dodging the fast-winded punches to the head. Moses screamed in pain after blocking a body punch that aimed for his rib cage using the same arm he blocked from the young warrior's punch the previous day. Ramses saw this as an advantage as he kicked Moses in his chest. The effect of the kick sent him flying backward as he landed on the mat hard for a second time. Moses could see the flashes again, but he sensed his brother approaching. He had to think of something quick or this would be the end of the challenge. Then he thought of what the young warrior said to him the other day.

Your brother is a heavy striker, but you have the best defense. Use that against him.

Ramses drew in close with his fists pumped ready to deliver the final blow. Moses kicked his feet up and struck Ramses on the bottom of his chin. Moses rolled back to his knees. *Oooohhh!* were the astonished sounds of the crowd as Ramses held his chin in both agony and fury. Moses got up to his feet closing in on Ramses while holding his guard. He could sense Ramses' frustration. Ramses turned and saw his brother engaging him.

"That's more like it," said Ramses. "Show me what you got."

Moses sensed multiple openings to deliver strikes on his brother. This was too easy. Ramses was toying with him. Moses decided to target the area that could weaken and slow down his arrogant brother. He faked a kick to Ramses' leg and struck at his stomach. Ramses deflected the punch and threw a jab of his own. Moses dodged it and threw a combo of punches towards his brother's body. Ramses deflected them as if he was swatting a fly and threw his forearm at Moses nearly cracking his jaw open. Moses landed on the mat for the third time. The crowd cheered screaming Ramses' name as he threw his arms up in celebration. In the corner of his eye, he could see the referee talking to the Grand Guardian.

"Your majesty, the boy is finished. I'm calling off the challenge."

The Grand Guardian threw up his hand shaking his head.

"Not yet. This fight is not over"

"But my lord, the boy is out cold. If we continue the challenge, Ramses might kill him."

The Grand Guardian gave him a fierce stare. The man nodded his head and stepped back on the platform.

What is the old man up to? questioned Ramses in his head.

Moses nearly blacked out as the ringing in his ears were the only sounds in his head. His vision was a blur. The flashes were like stars in the night sky. It was as if his destiny was fading. He began to see the nightmare again. His father choked out by the monster all over again in the throne room.

"I'm sorry fatha," he said in the vision. "I failed you. Ramses is the rightful chieftain."

"So… you give up that fast?" he said as the hand of the monster clenched his throat. "You will give up my legacy… that fast? The throne of Ezenwa? Will you truly allow your arrogant brother to be the very king that the people will trust to avenge me?"

Moses gasped as memories flashed in his head.

I bet you can't defeat me, said Ramses the day of Palesera's fall. *Master Ngozi taught me a new technique.*

I don't care what he taught you. I'm not afraid of you.

Then a recent memory flashed in his mind.

So the time has come I see, Ramses had said. *And this soon? I guess my reputation has grown exponentially enough for the Grand Guardian to show his face. It looks like it's time to turn things up, right little bro?*

Do not let your arrogance outweigh your judgment, were the words of Ngozi. *There's nothing worse in rulership than an arrogant king. An arrogant ruler always gets blind-sited by the enemy because he does not anticipate. In an arrogant man's eyes, he already has the victory of a battle that's uncertain.*

Then the revelation came back bubbling the surface of Moses' mind.

He might be bigger than me. He might be stronger than me. But one day I will be better than him.

Moses blinked his eyes open and sat up. The crowd was astonished by his resilience. Ramses gritted his teeth in a scowl. Moses felt a sharp pain in his jaw with liquid that had the taste of iron swimming around his saliva. He swallowed while getting back up to his feet. The man walked up to Moses bewildered.

"Are you okay to continue?" he asked.

Moses nodded.

The man turned back to the Grand Guardian and nodded. He backed away giving the boys space. This was going to be the outcome. Moses could sense it. Ramses could see it. Ramses threw up his hands. The arrogance and frustration sounded in his voice.

"Why didn't you stay down stupid fool? Onye nzuzu huh?"

Moses focused. The words of his brother meant nothing to him at this point.

"And you call yourself the son of Oba? You are weak. You were always weak. You are not even worthy to lick Fatha's shoes. I'm going to finish your ass off."

Moses scowled. His brother's words angered him. But he wasn't going to be in a blind rage. He took short breaths and had the thought of what Ngozi told him. *Do not let your emotions get the best of you. Instead, harness them. Use it as a weapon and not as a way of chaos.* Moses took a deep breath. Ramses howled using all his body weight to land a devastating blow to his little brother. Moses closed his eyes harnessing his anger to a source of energy. Ramses pumped his fist and delivered a powerful punch towards Moses' chest. Moses opened his eyes, feeling the energy channeling through him. He felt time freezing around him. He saw his brother delivering the punch in slow motion. The energy engulfed into sparks. Moses pumped his fists and threw a punch at Ramses' stomach. A combination of sparks and blue energy caved in Ramses' stomach knocking the wind out of him as he was sent flying nearly falling off the platform. The crowd was in complete silence as Ramses grunted and passed out.

The crowd cheered as everyone began to chant Moses' name. He smiled as the referee raised his hand as the victor.

"Here he is. Your new Chieftain of Ouidah, Moses Ezenwa!" yelled the man in the rose-colored blazer.

"Ekele dịrị onye isi ọhụụ! Hail to the new chief! Eze anyị ga-azọpụta anyị! Our king will save us!" yelled the crowd.

"Moses, you did it," said Korah. "Or should I say, your highness."

Moses smiled, lightly hitting his shoulder.

Korah placed his fist on his chest and bowed to Moses. He smiled and did the same. Korah raised his best friend's hand.

"Hail to the new Chieftain of Oudiah and soon to be High Chieftain of Nubariah!" Korah yelled.

The crowd cheered in an abrupt sound that shook the complex like an earthquake. Moses stared at Ngozi as he smiled nodding his head. The Grand Guardian got out of his seat and applauded Moses for his victory. The challenge was over. But his destiny was soon about to begin.

ACKNOWLEDGEMENTS

Although I am the author and creator of *Path of the Lion*, I cannot take all the credit without acknowledging those that contributed to this project and paved the way for this moment to happen.

First, I would like to thank the support of my family. I thank my wife for pushing me as well as supporting and loving me unconditionally since the moment we started dating back in 2013. I would like to also thank my sister Shalonda Johnson for telling me back in 2016 that I need to write about a black hero, including my wife who was my girlfriend at the time. The two of you literally pushed me to write about a black hero to either replace my original character Peter Tucker or add a black hero to the series. Hence in 2019, Moses Ezenwa was born. I thank my parents as well as siblings for their continuous support.

I would like to thank Mrs. Jerlean Noble and the Columbia Writers Alliance for building a platform to help support my novel. Mrs. Noble always believed in me and my writing career which gained the attention of Dr. Spearen who recruited me to the English program at Allen University back in 2012. I can't go without saying how grateful I am for Dr. Spearen to open the doors for me to receive my education and the contribution she made of honing my craft.

Now for the people who made this project physically possible. The first person I would like to thank is Geoff Herbach. You stuck with me on this project since day one when you mentored me in the winter residency of 2020 at Converse's MFA low residency program. I remembered later that summer when workshops and lectures moved virtual due to covid, you volunteered yourself to mentor me ensuring that the project flowed well with the beatpoints you helped me lay out. When I graduated with my MFA with the first half of the novel finalized, you could've disappeared, and I would be on my own with the second half of the novel. But you took time to continue to mentor me and provide feedback of what needs to be revised within each chapter. The novel was two years in the making, and I am in gratitude that I have met you and for you to mentor me.

Next, I would like to thank Macchiato Studios for their honesty and the original depictions of Moses and Ramses. I was blown away when I saw the drawings. From the start you guys were honest with your prices and never gave me a hard time when it came to understanding the vision.

Finally, I would also like to thank the illustrator of the phenomenal cover Nnamdi Peters. You truly depicted the art of Afrofuturism exceeding the vision that I had for the cover. Your art is truly legendary and I'm looking forward to working with you for more projects to come in the start of this franchise.

ABOUT THE AUTHOR

K.T. Brown is a self-published author and scholar who is a native South Carolinian born in Greenwood and raised in Columbia. He was always a passionate writer with a vivid imagination growing up as a young man. K.T. Brown graduated with a B.A. in English at Allen University and moved on to receive his MFA in Creative Writing at Converse University (formerly known as Converse College). He currently teaches English at Blackville Hilda High School in the Barnwell County Consolidated School District for 11th grade, 12th grade, and dual enrollment students as a consultant for Denmark Technical College. K.T. Brown currently lives in Orangeburg, SC with his wife Desiree and two children Hezekiah and Kyleah.

Path of the Lion

Rising Kingdom

Part Two: The Throne

Chapter Fifteen

A Dark Entity

Come, boy," said a mellow voice amid burning light.

Karungu, the heir of Thuku, followed the voice entering the burning light. He wore brown beads dressed in a white kaftan that sparkled.

"Come, boy… Come… come… I have everything you desire."

Karungu continued to follow the burning light with a curious mind. The light blinded him in milliseconds before a room full of gold was revealed to him. It was an unlimited amount of gold with gems glistening in blends. He was mesmerized by the unlimited wealth that was placed before him. He looked up and saw the burning light return but it shifted into a bright circle. Karungu was puzzled at the mysterious light.

"All this will be yours if you tap into your true nature and power," said the same voice through the light.

Karungu was still puzzled. What is his true nature? If only he knew his true power. Then another thought came up.

"My power is what I learned from my ancestors," said Karungu.

"Yet your father became powerless. Tell me. Is that the power you desire? Or do you want more? Be free from this curse and create your own destiny. It is set all around you. Unlimited wealth, power beyond your imagination."

Karungu stared at the gold and gemstones. The voice had a point. Karungu did not want to be held back. His mindset was to become Mombassa's greatest Chieftain. He drew to a stack of shinning gold and grabbed a handful of it enthralled by its touch.

"Got you right where I want you," said the voice as it grew more sinister.

Two black tendrils with the texture of gooey ink shot from out of the burning light and grabbed Karungu by the arms. The young man gasped using his strength the pull away from the dark tendrils, but they were too strong. Another tendril shot out and wrapped itself around Karungu. He looked down and saw the pure white of his kaftan stained in black oil. He felt another tendril catch hold of his throat. He gasped for air, but the atmosphere was closed from his esophagus. Karungu was desperate. He grabbed the tendril that gripped his neck trying to break free from the tight-fisted grip. Karungu could feel his body ascending to the light. Death and Hell were calling for him. He wanted to scream but couldn't. This was it. His eyes widened as the light grew brighter.

A long-winded gasp came out of the breath of Karungu as he sat up from his comforting bed. He peered at his surroundings and patted himself. He was not in Hell. It was a sigh of relief to him as he began to turn his focus on reality.

It has been seven years since he witnessed his father turning his back on his nation for the sake of his tribe. He'll never forget that day Ouidah fell to the Shadow League which caused a chain reaction of every tribe in Nubariah to be submissive to the Shadow Lords. Karungu was only a teen groomed to be both a man and leader to take his father's place as Jaguar Clan Chieftain. Witnessing that fatal day left him in a place of hopelessness. Watching his father make deals with the Shadow Lord of abiding by the laws and codes of the Shadow League in exchange for his people's liberty was baffling. *My father is a coward*, were the thoughts he tried to hide from his visage. If he was to take his father's place someday, he knew he had to become fiercer to lead his people.

Karungu summoned a couple of servants to freshen him in his personal washroom. It was the lavish treatment he was delighted to wake up to. The servants drenched him in his royal garment of leopard-spotted fur with a kaftan underneath. A gold chain was dangled over his neck as well as a gold digital watch. Karungu was officially in his reality, the lavish lifestyle into which he was born.

Once Karungu was dressed, he entered the palace halls of Lyayo, the Capital City of Mombassa. Lyayo was known as the Chrome City since the material for each building were made of solid chrome. Karungu walked down a path that led to a series of chambers. A woman stopped him in his tracks.

"You know your father is waiting for you in the council chambers," she said.

"I am aware of what father wants," said Karungu.

He turned around and faced the woman ignoring her Bantu braids and rose-colored lipstick.

"But I need to take care of something first."

"I know I am only your father's betrothed and not your mother, but I do care for you like a son. And I do care about your relationship with him. He may have made bad decisions as Chieftain, but he does mean well about your future."

"And that's the thing. You or Father know nothing of my well-being and how I feel. But you are right about one thing, he made a lot of bad decisions. Tell him I'll be there in a few minutes."

"Please don't keep him waiting Karungu. You know he's not a man of much patience."

Karungu turned from his father's betrothed and continued down the path leading to the chambers that were lined in rows. He entered a chamber that had an altar leading to a shrine. Burning incents were leaning within golden bowls in the shrine. A man in a beige kaftan wrapped in a turban matching his outfit was on his hands and knees praying in Swahili at the shrine. *"Mkubwa Ponyeni watu wetu. Iponye nchi yetu, ili tuwe kitu kimoja."* (Great Supreme heal our people. Heal our land, so we can become one). The man stood facing Karungu.

"I see that you are troubled young man," he said.

"Chief Priest I come to you to see if you can understand this dream I had last night," said Karungu.

The Priest nodded and gestured for the Jaguar Clan Prince to sit at a table near the altar. Karungu sat across the table from the Chief Priest. For a few seconds, there was silence.

"So tell me Karungu what bothers you?"

"I had a nightmare. It was pleasant for me in the beginning, but then things grew dark. I saw a burning light that led me to an unlimited amount of wealth. But then a voice told me that I must tap into my true nature and power to receive it. I embraced it at first, but then I was taken by three tendrils that came from the burning light. I was dragged to the light then I woke up here."

The Chief Priest was silent for a moment.

"Be careful of the decisions you make Karungu. We are living in dark times. Every choice we make has an impact on the people around us. You are the heir to the throne of Mombassa. A crucial moment will happen, and you alone will have to make a decision that will change the rest of your life."

"I see, but you didn't explain the tendrils and the burning light."

"If you had a dream of tendrils dragging you to a burning light then you are dealing with great deception. Perhaps your own heart is deceived. I did dream myself. I was shown by the Supreme that the dark entity is returning to join the Shadow Lords for the final war yet to come. Ekwenzu is looking for a new host. That dream you had is a warning Karungu. If you are tempted by your darkest impulse, you must turn from it quickly. Every man is capable of evil. But we also are capable of righteous acts. We all have decisions to make. Be sure to choose wisely Karungu."

The Jaguar Clan Prince rose to his feet and bowed to the Chief Priest.

"Thank you for bringing me clarity Chief Priest. I better get going. My father is waiting for me."

"The pleasure is all mine," said the Chief Priest.

Karungu walked out of the chamber to get to his father as the Chief Priest returned to the altar resuming his prayer.

Karungu rushed to the war chamber to meet with his father and his council. He slammed the wooden double doors open panting for air. His father and the council members stood to their feet giving him a disgusting look. Karungu stepped forth.

"Baba, my apologies for being…"

His father raised his hand to silence him. He was impatient. Karungu could tell by his scrunching lips.

"Save it, boy," he said. "You are the heir to my throne, and you arrive fifteen minutes late to an important meeting."

"But baba I…"

"Save it. Sit. There is much to discuss."

Karungu gave his father a quick glare and sat down. It was bad enough he was being scolded like a child at the age of 23, but for him unable to explain himself or have a say was getting to him. Karungu sat at the long table. The council sat along with his father. Karungu tried his best to draw back his temper. His lips were poked. He folded his hands on the table making himself appear to be engaged in his father's words as he continued the meeting.

"As I was saying before I was interrupted, there will be some changes made for Mombassa for our people to be more safe and secure. Now recently I made a deal with Emperor Mercius that will change the course of our territory. The Emperor agrees to withdraw his warriors from monitoring our cities and villages. We will now police our own people without interferences from outsiders."

The council in the chamber was cheering. Karungu curled his lips slightly with a smile. Conceivably his father finally did something right since Nubariah's destruction and the rise of the Bronze Empire. His father continued.

"In exchange for our military and militia to get re-educated in the dark arts."

"What!" yelled one of the council members.

Karungu was in a state of shock looking around at the baffled council.

"So, you're telling me that you are now selling out your military too!" questioned the council member.

Karungu stared at his father in utter confusion. He knew there was a catch to this. His father was helpless. It was too good to be true.

"Please, settle down," his father pleaded.

"How can we settle down with this outrage! It's bad enough our people are docile and lost their way of life. But now our military?"

"They will have an advantage..."

"But how? Once one practice the dark arts, there's no coming back. You can't wield both light and dark elements. You can only wield one power and quench the other. You might be scrambling for survival your highness, but the rest of us here are suffering. The Shadow Lord will soon set you up for your grave..."

"Enough!" yelled the Chieftain. "Nubariah is gone, and we have no leader to guide us in these times. The Bronze Empire has taken over and if we rebel now, our efforts will be buried along with our bodies. Compromise is the only answer to stay in power and lead our people to a new age."

Karungu leaned back peering around the council and his father. Another council member opened his mouth to speak.

"I say we put this decision to a vote."

"This is not a democracy!" yelled the Chieftain banging his fist on the table. "We have no choice but to follow the Emperor or face death."

"We're dying anyway as a people. All favor of vetoing the military re-education initiative say "I"."

The entire council raised their hands with "I's". Karungu was hesitant glancing at his father who scowled at him, but he raised his hand saying, "I".

His father scowled.

"You don't know what you're getting your into," he said. Emperor Mercius is ruthless. He can cause a mass genocide in seconds."

"We must gain back our honor," said the council member. "Chieftain Oba died with his."

Karungu watched as his father stormed out of the chamber without a word. He felt a hand touch his shoulder.

"Your father is a good man," the council member said. "He means well for his people, but he's doing this the wrong way. Have faith in your father."

Karungu dropped his head. *Why keep making excuses for him*, he thought. Karungu stood to his feet.

"Looks like this meeting is adjourned," he said. "I will now retire back to my chambers for now."